T-REX

ALAN SPENCER

SEVERED PRESS
HOBART TASMANIA

T-REX

PROLOGUE

All you need is your big break. You can't start at the top. I may be in the gutter, but I'm sure as hell not in the sewer. I don't have to work with A-listers right from the start. Place me in front of a camera and film me, baby. That's what I really want. You got to climb the rungs of the industry ladder to get somewhere. This is Hollywood from the bleacher seats. Call me a roughneck actor. Grit, blood, sweat, and poverty, baby.

I'll get a SAG card for this stupid movie. This'll lead to other things. Better things. The world will see my face on cable TV, and they'll know Mark Rodman has finally arrived. The audience will want more Rodman. They'll demand Rodman until they get their fill of me. And by then, I'll be a millionaire.

The same encouraging sentences repeated in Mark Rodman's head throughout the long trip across the ocean. He was combating nerves and questioning his choice in participating in the film *Dino Buffet 3: Gorgers*. The term "career killer" kept popping up in his head alongside "this could be the biggest mistake of your life".

There was more going on in Mark's mind than movie jitters. The concerns really set in after he pulled the boat ashore. Saying he screwed this gig up was the understatement of the year.

When the crew of thirty-five persons unloaded from the big boat, Mark excused himself from the crowd. He stepped beyond the white sandy beach, trudged up a hill, and stood on top of a rock ledge. He overlooked the crystal blue Caribbean ocean and really hashed out the problem banging around in his head.

The issue was easy to identify.

He lied to director Bruce Ryder.

If he could work through that lie, maybe, just maybe, he could enjoy his first acting job. It could serve as a fun story to tell his kids when he finally had them. The lie was simple and had snowballed into something colossal.

Take it from the top, man. Hash through it. Think it out, baby.

Mark tried to dissect the situation.

It wasn't good from any angle.

He watched the various actors and small crew lift up a blue canopy onto four poles to create a shaded break area. The crew were opening coolers and setting up for a late lunch before today's film shooting began.

You have to figure this out for these people.

You've put them all in danger.

Just take it from the top.

There was an open casting call for the movie *Dino Buffet 3: Gorgers* two weeks ago. He auditioned for the part of Surfer Friend #2. He was perfect for the role. He had long blonde hair that ran down to his shoulders. He had the surfer's physique. He wore neon green rimmed glasses. Mark was cool 80's all the way, baby. That day, he dressed in a bright shirt with the sleeves ripped out and tight cargo pants. He added another touch that he knew would win over the director. Mark hit the tanning salon and kept his sunglasses on to create tan lines on his face. He was now a true surfer dude. Every other word out of his mouth was *dude, man, boss, tubular, Rastafarian, awe-some,* and *groovy*. In the business, they called it method acting.

The audition was held in an empty high school auditorium in Tampa, Florida. The line of hopefuls ran all the way outside the front doors. During the audition, Bruce Ryder, the big director himself, didn't seem at all interested in his method surfer act. The hotshot gave him a sigh, an eye roll, and a tepid, "*We'll let you know. The door's on your left.*"

On his way out, Mark accidentally dropped his wallet. He dropped it just right so that his left foot kicked it at Bruce's sandaled feet. The director picked up the wallet. It was open, showing his driver's license and a picture of his father's fishing boat.

The director's attitude changed instantly. He removed the picture of the boat and held it up to Mark. "You know anything about boats?"

"Sure, man. I've sailed all my life. My father owns several boats. He taught me everything I know."

The director ignored most of what he said. "So you can sail? Can you borrow your dad's boat?"

Before he realized it, Mark had volunteered himself to sail the cast and crew on his father's boat to an undisclosed island. After he agreed, Bruce Ryder promised him the part of Surfer Friend #2.

He didn't have a problem doing the director a favor. And what was the big deal anyway? Mark knew how to sail. His grandfather was a commercial fisherman, and his father was a stock market champion who owned a whole fleet of boats, and Mark had played captain on all of them growing up.

Sailing wasn't the problem.

Borrowing the boat wasn't a problem.

Navigating was the problem.

Bruce Ryder handed him a map this morning and said, "Take us to Pagoda Island. I'm going downstairs to get drunk and play with Candy. Do not disturb me."

Mark thought he was reading the map correctly. After hours of scrunching his brow and drinking one too many of the beers flowing between the various crew on the top deck of the boat, he realized he was lost. Drunk, nervous, or just plain stupid, he had put everybody in a bad position.

The nervous hours of sailing passed, and he kept heading towards a nothing horizon on the ocean. He was about to break down and cry and tell everybody the truth when an island finally did appear. He didn't know if it was Pagoda Island. Mark wasn't sure how the hell they would get back home. Sure, he could use the radio and call for help, but would he get himself fired from the acting role if he admitted his mistake?

The tiny voice in the back of his head kept saying, *Tell them after you're done shooting. This is your shot. It may be your only shot. Get in front of that camera, get your screen time, and go from there. And maybe, just maybe, you can get them home after all. You're all worked up over nothing. It's an island. For all I know, this could be Pagoda Island. It might not be, but so what? I'll get them home. I know I will. Relax. Slow your roll, baby.*

Mark kept his gaze on the crew along the beach. They were enjoying their cooler lunch of cold cut sandwiches and sodas. After thinking for a while longer, he decided it was best to keep his mouth shut. Things would work out. He needed a moment to clear his head, and he did that. Mission accomplished. Groovy.

His bladder ached. He downed he couldn't remember how many beers on the way to this mystery island. The ground was a mix of sand and dirt the farther he walked away from the beach. He entered the edge of what appeared to be a dense collection of trees that went on and on for miles. The trees were a hybrid of palm trees and sap bearing trees. The bark along many of the trees were wet with syrup. Bugs were crawling over the tree to enjoy the golden brown sticky stuff.

The bugs themselves were very strange. He imagined a rhinoceros beetle matched with thick leathery wings. They were hulking. Double the size of his thumb, if not bigger. He'd hate to have those suckers crawling all over him. Would they eat his flesh or inject him with poison?

Don't think about it, baby.

He searched for a tree that didn't have sap or bugs covering it. He imagined whipping his thing out and one of those nasty insects crawling up into his peter.

No thanks. I've watched too many documentaries on the Discovery channel. This kind of stuff really does happen.

After relieving himself, he felt a vibration at his feet. It sounded like two loud stomps, and then a low growl. He couldn't make sense of the noises. It would take a semi-truck, a real diesel engine, to come even close.

He heard trees creak and bend. The steps were spread out and quieter the longer they carried on. Something was trying to sneak up on him. When he turned around fast, he gasped at the standing towering creature twenty yards out from him.

The size, the enormity, the impossibility of its existence, it had Mark taking off in a mad sprint. He fled deeper into the thick of trees. He didn't know which way he had come from or which way to go. He was lost with no idea of where to turn next. The foliage varied. He imagined a rain forest, met with paradise, met with a bad science fiction movie. Giant oversized plants and green pods that looked like they could open up and eat you like a Venus flytrap were everywhere.

Mark vaulted faster. He was out of breath, but he had all the motivation in the world to keep picking up speed. He dodged a neon blue crab creature the size of a dog. It snapped its pincers and came half an inch from snapping off his arm.

Where have I taken these people?

I have to go back and warn them.

Everybody's in danger.

THIS CAN'T BE HAPPENING!

The giant beast was stomping after him. Trees were punched and in half like nothing twigs. Debris was flying in all directions; even crashing ahead of him from the sheer force of the creature's blows. He was the prey in the game of cat and mouse, and the way things were going, he was most certainly going to lose this game.

One hope waited up ahead.

A running stream with frothy burbling water appeared nearby. That stream carried on for a short distance and abruptly changed into an enormous waterfall. That was his best shot.

The beast was closing in.

Mark didn't think.

He braced his body and leaped off of the edge of the waterfall. He didn't know what lay below, or how far the drop would be, or what that fall would do to him. Death was a high probability.

He was in the air and falling fast.

He was free of the beast.

Or so he thought!

The enormous monster eclipsed everything around him in shadow. He wasn't careening towards the water two-stories down anymore. He was getting lost in the black hole closing in on him. The T-Rex had taken a dive off the edge right with him.

Mark was spattered with a coating of heavy rubber glue-like saliva. The hot breath was a noxious belch from the deepest sulfur pits of hell. The beast snapped its mouth closed. He was inside its mouth up to the neck. His head was decapitated by the bite-down. The would-be actor's head did a wild bowling ball spin and plunged into the waters below. The rest of his body went down the T-Rex's hungry throat in one greedy gulp.

PART ONE

MR. DIRECTOR

While Mark Rodman's body was being digested by boiling hot digestive enzymes, Bruce Ryder was enjoying a deep alcohol-induced slumber at the bottom level of the borrowed boat. The easy sway of the water made it so easy to sleep. He could've slept during the entire three-day shooting schedule on the island if it weren't for the soft, sexy voice of his long-time girlfriend speaking to him.

Candy Sweet had that kind of silky voice. The words were simple, yet heavy with sex. He didn't open his eyes. He listened to her. The way Candy spoke, she could get a corpse hard.

"Oh Bruce Bruce. You need to wake up."

"A little longer, baby."

"My sweet little man needs to wake up. Won't you wake up for me, baby? Huh, my big man? Won't you *rise* for me? I know my Bruce Bruce is tired. Can you be a big man and get up for me?"

He groaned, "Come back in an hour, sweetheart."

"You said that two hours ago."

"I know. One more hour. Please. My head is killing me."

That much was true. It felt like somebody had dropped an anvil on his head and dipped his liver in vinegar.

"The actors are eating all the food and drinking all the beer."

"Huh? They're doing what? Why didn't you tell me sooner? *Crap.*"

Bruce lunged out of bed. They couldn't eat all the food. It had to be rationed out over the next three days. He didn't have any other means of procuring food. There were no grocery stores to visit; not that would matter. He didn't have the budget to replenish any of the food stock. Didn't these idiot actors know this?

He had to think fast.

He told Candy Sweet to get Blast on it. The special effects guy was good at being an authority when Bruce was either too drunk or too busy to handle a crew acting up.

Candy rushed back up to the main deck to tell Blast what to do. He could hear her graceful porno girl steps glide off the boat and onto the beach.

He was alone again. He would have to get himself together and fast. If the director didn't get the crew in line from the start, the movie would go down in flames. The actors would consider him a pushover and question his authority. He couldn't afford any hiccups. When it came to low budget moviemaking, it was a world of one takes, lightening quick schedules, and no money to fix issues.

Wake up. Do your thing. You're in control. Take the reigns. You're Bruce Ryder. Start acting like it.

Bruce trudged over to the corner sink and splashed his face. The cold water wasn't enough to perk him up. Three cigarettes and a shot of bourbon later, he was getting there.

He showered and slipped on a pair of tattered jeans and a faded Bon Jovi t-shirt. He worked his long dyed black hair into a ponytail. He made sure his beard color matched his hair. There were slight gray roots coming in on his face, but there wasn't time to fix it. He knew he wasn't fooling anybody. He was fifty-eight years old and trying to look twenty-five. The attempt to look young was what Candy would lovingly call "cute" for a man his age.

He clutched his big belly and sighed. He was an old, greasy, washed up director. Some would call it pathetic. He wouldn't, and that's all that mattered. He loved making movies, period. If anybody had a problem with the work he churned out, they could ride a hot air balloon up his ass.

His career was a sordid one. He rode the porno wave in the '80's. He made over sixty skin films. When it came to the adult film industry, he didn't have to cut film anymore. This was all shot-on-video. Ultra cheap. All he needed was a lighting crew, a boom guy, and some people to have sex with each other.

The nineties were a different game. He got out of the bedroom and into the open air. He started to make low budget action movies while riding the novelty of having famous porn stars act in them. The gimmick worked magnificently. He went on to direct various slasher movies like *Lake Slash*, *Body Bag High*, *Hay Ride Massacre*, *Dracula Hunt*, and *Death Dialer*. What he couldn't deliver on special effects, he more than made up for it with tits and ass by the pound.

The industry changed yet again in the 2000's. The market shifted. Horror movies weren't as lucrative anymore. Now, it was CGI creature features and science fiction cheapies made for cable that did the trick. All these movies required was a washed up movie star and a CGI monster. He had both for *Dino Buffet 3: Gorgers*. And to top it off, he still had the tits and ass to back it all up. The movie would make itself. He would shoot the dinosaur island scenes in the coming three days, and the rest of the story could be shot back in Florida.

Bruce could lie to the producers who were funding this film, but he couldn't lie to himself. He farted out the script for *Dino Buffet 3*. The story went like this: a boat of partying twenty somethings get lost on the ocean and end up on an island where the government has kept secret their biggest weapon: a dozen T-Rexes. Unbeknownst to the world, the T-Rexes were being trained to fight ISIS through a convoluted, ridiculous process. The only problem, these dinos didn't want to eat only terrorists' flesh. They wanted to devour ALL flesh, and these twenty-somethings were in for a night of true terror. Commence the dino buffet.

The director had an easy plan. After shooting these fresh-faced youngsters running from nothing throughout the woods for the next three days, he would go back to his studio in Tampa and add CGI dinosaurs and gore. What he wouldn't later add was the nudity. He had four porno girls including his longtime girlfriend, Candy Sweet, ready to drop their tops and show the camera their wonderful globes. He might as well call the movie *Dino Buffet 3: Lost in Fun Bag Island.*

The Ryder magic machine was churning bronze. He wasn't big time. Screw the bad reviews and the jokes made at his expense. He was a working director. It was a paycheck. If you didn't like it, there was that hot air balloon ride you could take.

The movie was getting off to a great start despite the current situation. Sure, he needed to sober up quick and shoot a few scenes and stop the crew from devouring their food supplies. Once the ball got rolling, it wouldn't stop.

He lit a cigarette and stepped upstairs to the main deck and then walked down the stairs extended from the side of the boat. His hangover was getting better. His head wasn't killing him anymore.

He was starting to feel really good about this movie.

Nothing bad can happen, he thought.

HAVE A BLAST

Henry "Blast" Porter did his best to get the twenty-two-person crew in line. They were still drunk from the partying they did on the boat. The director was nowhere in sight. He couldn't blame Bruce for wanting to dip his wick in Candy Sweet. She was a pretty piece of tail. Nobody would get a lick of work out of Blast if he was married to *that* woman. But that wasn't Blast's situation. He focused on the real issue. This had turned into a booze cruise instead of a movie shoot. That had to stop and quick.

If that fat ass would get out of bed, he could get these idiots in line.

I've tried to level with them. I told them Bruce wouldn't approve of this and they ignored me. They think I'm a joke. I can only imagine what else they think of me. The way those young punks and valley girl bitches look at me sometimes, they think I'm a washed-up loser. They laugh at me when I'm gone. I know it.

I'll show them who's a joke.

Yeah.

They won't be laughing in a minute.

I'll teach them a real good lesson.

He stomped away from underneath the canopy where everybody was eating, drinking, and joking around. The scene could've doubled as a frat party. Mindy Duncan was pouring beer over Chris Toddy's head. Joey Mingle and David Perkins were playing baseball by using beer cans and a stick they found on the beach. Helen Kidd and Eddie Lumley had snuck off to have sex. He could smell the hormones exude off the pretty young people.

They won't listen to me, but they'll listen to something else.

He was a special effects guy. He created practical effects and doubled as lighting and boom guy when needed. Blast thrived in the '80's when horror movies were churned out at a hundred miles an hour, and now he survived on a threadbare basis working with Bruce Ryder. He was grateful to still be doing his craft at the age of forty-five. But he wasn't here to babysit horny youngsters who didn't respect having a job in the industry.

He was here to do a job.

Bottom line.

Blast skulked off to a corner under a small set of palm trees where he set up his work station. He had a fold out table up. On top of it were four boxes heaping full with rubber limbs and human pieces. Underneath the table, he had his make-up kit and what he called his "slaughter simulation" tackle box full of glues, appliances, and random tools he needed to create fast effects for cheap. He couldn't forget the biggest necessity: four huge plastic jugs of fake blood and gelatin guts. He used gelatin instead of actual slaughterhouse guts to avoid the terrible smell. Among the items, he also kept a 9mm pistol.

He double checked the 9mm for bullets.

She was fully loaded.

I'll scare some sense into them.

They'll see my steel and poop.

Wave this baby around, and they'll respect me.

I'll shoot a round into the air and get their attention.

Let's do this!

"Whoa, hold up!" Bruce snatched the 9mm out of his hands. "I'm not going to ask you what you were going to do with that. Just put that bad boy back where you found it. End of story. You got to promise me not to bring that thing back out again, you got me?

"We go back a long time, Blast. I know these kids are out of control. They're not professionals. They think acting's a breeze. By the end of our three days, they'll be new people. Some will bow out and never be in a movie again, and others, they'll keep on acting with new vigor. Thanks for trying to tame the herd. I owe you one, Blast. I'm giving you a bonus."

Blast went from snarling mad to laughing. "And how much is that bonus?"

"A three percent cut from the gross DVD profits we make in Japan. How's that?"

"Basically, a case of beer and a hearty handshake."

"I'd be grateful if I were you. I don't hand out bonuses. Not even to myself."

Blast put the 9mm back into the box. "Believe me, I know you don't. I'm grateful. I'm honored."

"Good." The director held up his arms and marveled at the surroundings. "This island is really something. Very tropical, and very free of charge. I'm glad the studio gave us this lead. Nobody owns it. Pagoda Island will be cheaper to shoot on than in the Philippines and a lot less dangerous. It's perfect. I might shoot parts four and five here too."

"You signed a deal for two more *Dino Buffets*?"

"You betcha. These dinosaurs are hungry, and they're going to eat. Now follow me. There's no time to lose. It's time for one of my cast and crew speeches."

Oh God, Blast thought. *Not another one of his speeches. I've heard the same speech five hundred times.*

"Are you sure I shouldn't take my 9mm with me?"

The director gave him a crooked smile. "Hah hah. Very funny. Nothing can go wrong on this shoot. We've got a tight schedule. I need you sharp. And unarmed."

"You got it, boss."

"That's what I like to hear. Now help me wrangle up everybody under the canopy. I'll give them the brief version of my speech. I'll go easy on them."

"Thank God for small favors. Bruce Ryder, the merciful!"

THE RYDER SPEECH

Shortly after actors Helen Kidd and Eddie Lumley returned from the woods after their sexual romp, Blast, Candy, and Bruce gathered the crew under the big canopy. The thought of the two actors banging made Bruce laugh to himself as he studied the actors who were doing exactly as he told them to do before they set sail, and that was to get in character by getting drunk, horny, and stupid. He should've told Blast about that plan. That might've saved the special effects maestro's blood pressure from spiking.

The minor 9mm hiccup aside, he was proud of himself for spending the extra money on booze, because this bunch couldn't act. If he was going to get a half-way respectable product out of this, he would have to deliver a speech that would make Shakespeare want to hang it up for good.

He had his one speech.

The speech of all speeches.

Bruce gave Candy Sweet a loving glance before speaking. He wanted to marry this woman. He knew all about flings and movie set romances, and Candy Sweet wasn't either of those. Her long natural blonde hair, natural double d tits, and the Angelina Jolie lips and Pamela Anderson bubbly girl attitude stirred up many things in this old man that no other woman could. Candy Sweet was the ultimate babe. Once this movie was over and *Dino Buffet 3* premiered on cable, they would watch it with their friends, and that's when he would propose to her.

That would be a different speech altogether.

This speech was business.

"Thank you all for signing on for the film. I have a few things to cover before we get to work. First thing, I know some of you people want to call me a smut peddler or a second rate crap-fest movie man who is overly obsessed with the female mammary gland. That's fine. It's accurate. Go ahead. Call me a hack. Dub me a smut king. A B movie loser. Say I'm washed up. Get it out of your systems. I'm serious. Go ahead. Take your best shot. Really. Do it. Let me have it. I know I deserve it."

Candy Sweet got the ball rolling, because no newbie actor trusted it when a director made this request.

"Washed up loser," Candy smiled big. "A second grader could write better scripts than you, buddy. I'd rather have my kneecaps broken than watch one of your movies again. Your movies are turds."

The drunk cast got the message. Their collective words hit him as a drunken barrage of joyful punch lines and criticisms. This lasted a good five minutes. The last line from Candy, who made her voice intentionally louder than everybody else's, said, "Your movies suck hairy balls."

Bruce clapped his hands together once. "Okay. Wasn't that fun?"

Everybody agreed that yes, that was *very* fun.

"I do this to not only humble myself, but to let you know I'm aware we're making an ultra cheap trash film. I'm okay with that, and you should be too. You're working. You're in front of the camera. You're doing your best to achieve your dreams. It's a great thing.

"Real quick, I started in this business by a happy accident. I was in my early twenties. I dropped out of film school. I was broke and unemployed. I shared an apartment with another aspiring film student. Then destiny happens. There's a knock on our door. I open it up, and there's this guy who looks like a used car salesman, and he talks like one too. He asks me this one question. This one question got the ball rolling in my career, and I haven't looked back ever since.

"That question was a rather simple one. *Can you hold a light over two people fucking for about ten to fifteen minutes?* I said, Hell- yeah, I could! I went next door to the porno shoot in progress. I held that light over two people fucking for ten to fifteen minutes. I had unknowingly replaced a crewmember who had walked off the set because his values were being tested.

"Throughout my career being a crewmember, scriptwriter, and a director, I've followed a specific set of rules. Know who you are and what you make and accept that. If you're okay with what you do, and you have fun, then great. Who cares if you win an Academy Award or not?

"That porn director who gave me my start offered me some words to live by. He simply said, "Bruce, there's one thing that has kept me thriving in this business. You can't always read between the lines, but you can most certainly read between the legs." What he meant, of course, was not to take yourself too seriously.

"So as far as you beautiful, charismatic people are concerned, I say this to you. You signed on for this project. I told you exactly what you'd be doing, how you'd be doing it, and how much you'd get paid to do the said above. I don't trick people or lie to you; I don't coerce people with bullshit Hollywood glamour talk to get what I want. I expect you to deliver your side of the contract. Have fun, put in your work, and make the best out of this low budget experience. Imagine it being a fun camping trip. Now I want a hundred percent from you people. Okay, let's get organized."

Candy helped him gather fifteen of the actors, and together they unloaded beach chairs, rolled out beach towels, and put up a volleyball net.

The director told everybody what was happening. "Everything gets in position. This is the scene set-up. You're on an island. You're lost, drunk, and suddenly realizing this is a beautiful day. So why not have fun?"

Bruce got the camera operator and the boom man in place. He didn't need the extensive crews the other productions required. This was the bare bones of the skeleton.

The scene in progress was the padding of the film. He would insert a good five minute shot of these young idiots spiking, serving, and diving for the volleyball. Anything to reach the ninety-minute mark.

Candy was hamming it up during the volleyball game. She wore that tight lime green bikini and stuck out her giant shiny globe breasts freshly covered in baby oil, giggled when she chased after the ball, bent over to show that g-string butt floss action, and flirted with the guys. This entailed a lot of licking of the lips and laughing overmuch at things that were mildly to not funny at all.

"You spiked it so hard!"

"Wait, Chad, show me how to hit the ball?"

"Guys, what's the score again?"

"I feel like my sunscreen's wearing off. You should rub some on me later, Brad."

"Did you see that? Bobby hit it so hard he about busted the ball!"

"Oh my! I keep hitting the ball into the net."

God love her, Bruce thought. She was giving a hundred and ten percent. God love her again, because she couldn't act worth a damn. Even by *Baywatch* standards. The funny thing, the audience still loved her. She was fucking cute.

The porn queen had starred in all twelve *Suck It* films. She also had roles in *Sloppy Firsts, Sloppy Seconds, Sloppy Thirds,* and the conclusion of the *Sloppy* series, *Sloppy Fourths.* Then there was the ultra hit, *Stay Hard* that was a *Die Hard* rip-off featuring hardcore sex.

All of this was courtesy of Bruce Ryder and his production company. He made hardcore films again for a brief period when normal movie work had dried up in the early 2000's. Thank God for that short lived return because he wouldn't have met his favorite lady.

Candy Sweet was obviously older than the rest of the eighteen to twenty-five-year-old crew. She had turned the dreaded thirty a couple of months ago. She was gorgeous and remained a bombshell, but she could no longer pass as that fresh out of high school and stepping into college kind of girl. He didn't care. She had the goods and delivered them.

The director kept the scene rolling. They played volleyball for another fifteen minutes without stopping. That should be enough padding, he thought.

"Cut! Great job everybody. I love your energy. Now let's shoot the gory beach scene."

BLOOD BEACH

Squirt a little more on that, and let's call you dead.

Blast was on his haunches. He shoved a severed woman's head made of latex with its wet mop of fake blonde hair into the sand. He rubbed a version of KY Jelly along the rubber face called *Good Goo* to make the skin shiny and more lifelike. The final step, he took his fast food ketchup container—the one with the tiny hole at the tip to make a squirting sound—and slathered the head with fake blood. He sprayed around the sand liberally to simulate real dinosaur wound blood spatter.

He covered a large section of the beach in human pieces. The parts from fifty people were spread out along the special section of the beach. From a distance, it might look like a successful massacre. Up close, people would think a dime store Halloween shop had been pummeled by a tornado.

Bruce called out from his beach volleyball scene in progress, "You almost done over there, Blast?"

"Another ten minutes. Finishing touches."

"Gotcha. Ten minutes."

The director was angling around the volleyball game getting his bouncing and jiggling shots. Candy was doing the most with her body. He envied the old bastard. Bruce was living the good life. All the glory to him, he thought. The bastard was as ugly as a troll, but his dick lived like a handsome hunk.

And this is my glory. Blast hurried over to his effects table. He dragged out the plastic bucket full of gelatin guts. Long intestines, livers, spleens, hearts—everything inside the body the gory fans wanted to see, he would supply it in dripping fashion.

The method was simple. Take each of the gelatin guts and dip into the blood bucket once, hold for ten seconds, and scatter them between the fake body parts. Take. Dip. Hold. Spread. Repeat. He did this until Bruce called out to him again.

"Ready over there?"

"It's a go."

"Good. Give us another minute. We're taking down the volleyball net and moving the chairs so these kids can get a running start towards the death and dismemberment."

Blast didn't hear the director.

In the corner of his eyes, he swore he saw something.

Not something.

Somebody.

There was the beach, and then there was the line where the beach stopped and the palms trees began. Between the trees, he swore he saw a head peek out and then quickly dart away.

Maybe he was working under the sun too long.

Maybe he was staring at dead dummy heads for too long.

You need to hydrate.

You're seeing things.

Blast returned to his table for a drink of bottled water and a chance to catch his breath. He had been going hard at it to keep up with Bruce's schedule. He wasn't as young as he used to be.

Yeah, he thought. He was only seeing things.

That had to be it.

MAN IN THE FOREST

He saw me.

Hide.

No.

Stay where you are.

You have nothing to be afraid of here. This is your home. It will remain your home. Nobody can take you away from here. If they try, you'll know what to do.

Why are they here? They'll bring others. When there's one group of people, another one will be right behind them.

I can't kill them all. I'm outnumbered. One at a time is one thing, but this many at once, I'm not so sure.

You have to kill them. You realize that, don't you? You can't risk the word getting out that you're here hiding out. If anybody tells anybody about this place, it's over. They'll find out you're here, who you are, and where you should be, and I won't be put into any damn padded room. I'll kill myself first.

No. That won't be necessary. You're going to have to kill them all before they leave the island. It's that easy. They can't leave.

They won't.

They won't.

They won't.

This doesn't have to be a problem. There's plenty of beautiful flesh to enjoy for everyone here. Enough skin even for my special purposes. They're all so lovely. I want their skin so bad.

No, no, no, no, this doesn't have to be a bad thing.
He didn't see me.
He went back to work.
Very good.
Nobody knows about me.
My friends will be very happy they have something new to hunt.
I'm so very ready to play with flesh.

SCREAM!

"On your marks. Get set. *Goooooooo!*"

Bruce loved this moment. It was one of the main reasons he wanted to be a B movie director. He watched the horde of bikini and shorts clad actors sprint across the beach in terror. His cameraman was capturing it all with his handheld steady cam.

He gave them on-the-spot directions.

"Scream! Yes, yes, yes! Faster! Turn around. Pretend a big T-Rex is behind you. He's stomping his way closer. Oh no. Watch out. Turn around, see it coming, and run faster. Scream again! Really hit those notes. Really blast out our eardrums. The only thing you're thinking about is how close that giant mouth is from taking a big bite out or your ass. And, oh no! The beach ahead of you is littered with human pieces. Your friends are in bits! Dear God, they're all dead. No more fun! It's nasty! It's ghastly! Oh, the humanity! SCREAM! RUN!

"Now there are three more dinosaurs after you. Big ugly green ones the size of Pittsburgh. Doug, jump up like you just dodged getting bit by an inch. Yeah! Perfect! Everybody keep it going. Terror. Fear. Dinosaurs!

"Dart around the body parts. It's okay, Darlene. You stepped on a severed head. Now shamble around like you've twisted your ankle. Now fall. Stay there and keep screaming. The dinosaurs got you. Now lay there dead. Everybody else, don't stop running.

Keep moving. Look terrified. You're going to die! *Dinos! Dinos! Dinos! Dinos! And cut!*

"Wonderful. Everybody go back to the starting line. I'll let you catch your breaths, and we'll do that scene one more time. Darlene, I want you to trip over the same severed head like you did a moment ago. Todd, I want you and Adrienne to fall, scream, and thrash around like you're being eaten by a dinosaur, and then lay still like you're dead on my cue. Very good. This is turning out so perfect, guys."

Bruce thanked his camera operator, Eric Joyce, and stepped aside to have a cigarette. He didn't notice the actress standing there behind him until he turned completely around.

He couldn't read her expression. "Hi there. What's on your mind? You didn't get hurt doing that scene? It'd be easy to twist an ankle on the sand."

He knew his cast and crew by name. This was Zoe Carmichael. She was a great piece of eye candy for the film. She wore a two-piece hot pink bikini. Her breasts were milky and fat, and her nipples were popping like buttons. Her black hair hung down in her face from a gust of wind, and she had to peel a strand of it from her cinnamon colored lips. She couldn't have been more than a hundred and ten pounds and barely nineteen. He had a smoking hot cast in this movie. Even the guys were hunks. Bruce wasn't sure how he got so lucky. It helped he actually held real auditions this time.

Zoe started talking in her valley girl voice.

"Like, I wanted to ask you a few questions. Um, yeah, why are there dinosaurs here? I mean, aren't they extinct? And, um, you know, like, why hasn't anybody found out there are dinosaurs on this island by now? Wouldn't somebody on accident have stumbled upon it already? And how could the government control the dinosaurs? And I was thinking, if this island was a training base for dinosaurs to fight terrorism, how would you get the dinosaurs from here to like, I don't know, Baghdad or wherever in the Middle East, without anybody finding out? And once they did fight ISIS, or whoever, wouldn't people find out the government had been holding back the greatest scientific discovery in centuries? And why, Mr. Director, haven't I had a scene where I take my top off yet?"

Well, all right. This girl definitely wants to be in a Bruce Ryder film.

"Well, those scenes are coming up just after this one, and I'd be happy to adjust the script so we can accommodate you. I know you weren't originally slated for those scenes, but I can have a contract written up."

He didn't see it coming, and even if he did, he didn't have the quick instinct to dodge or duck. Zoe bunched up that tiny cute fist and drove it home right into his face. He thought he was dealing with a prize fighter trying to throw a TKO punch. He was thrown off of his feet. His head was cocked back, and his eyeballs were spinning in their sockets.

He slammed against the beach onto his back with a grunt. Blood gushed from his nose. He was seeing double. Two Zoe figures were standing over him huffing and angry. She didn't sound so valley girl anymore.

She was suddenly very articulate when she growled, "You remember *Dodo Attack: Rise from Extinction*? Probably not, you talentless shit bag. You use women and throw them away. We're people. We have feelings. Not to you, you sleazebag. We're just packages you want to unwrap and exploit for your benefit.

"That's what you did to my sister, Angie Carmichael. She was in your stupid *Dodo* movie, and you made her show her tits when she didn't want to. What you did to my sister, what she went through, you have no idea because you don't care about people. A normal, thinking, feeling person would, but you, you're a subhuman ass pony. I'd stomp on you, but you'd probably get a sexual thrill from it, you perv."

Before Bruce recovered from the blow, Candy Sweet had rushed across the beach, grabbed Zoe by the arm, and forced her across the other side of the beach for a talk.

Blast was helping him up from the ground. "Wow. I totally saw that. She punched your face in. Damn, man."

"My nose is bleeding like a faucet. Man, she tricked me. She set me up to say something about boobs and wham-o! Fist city."

Blast handed him a rag. "Stop the blood with this."

The director pressed it to his nose. "Now I remember. Angie Carmichael. *Dodo Attack*, yeah, yeah, yeah. But I don't get it. You remember Angie?"

Blast's eyes widened, and then he grinned like a cartoon jackal. He put his hands up to his chest to shape huge breasts. "Yeah. Angie Carmichael. Yeah. Oh man. Real stacked. Smoking hot tits. You betcha I remember Angie Carmichael."

The director's shock was changing into consternation. "I recall Angie being more than willing to drop her top. I didn't talk her into anything. It was contracted and discussed. I hate it when women try to turn me into a bad guy. I never trick anybody. I never ask anybody to do something they don't want to do. It's all contracted and in print as clear as the sun is in the sky. Zoe's got me wrong. And the bitch punched me in the nose. And here I thought the shoot was going so well."

"Don't worry, director. Your lady will set things straight."

"That's why I love her. Candy always knows what to do, and you never have to ask. I don't think anybody else saw this happen. Would you help me scramble the right ladies for the lesbian waterfall make out scenes? I don't want to lose shooting time."

Blast smiled. "Got it. I have zero qualms with helping you out with the lesbian waterfall make out scene, Mr. Director."

CANDY SWEET, DIPLOMAT

Candy had to deal with the situation and quick. She saw Zoe's punch and Bruce go down hard. What else this crazy girl would do was yet to be seen. Candy wouldn't give her another chance to touch her man. She grabbed Zoe's arm and forced her across the other side of the beach as far away from Bruce as possible.

Zoe wasn't happy. She thrashed and tried to slip from Candy's hold. "Let me go you porno bitch. You have no right to touch me. Skank, stop!"

You want to hit her. Be patient. She's already worked up. You hit her, she'll go off even more. "No more fighting. Calm down. I want to hear your side if you let me. And I got things to say too."

"Bitch, I don't need you to talk to me! I have nothing to say to you or any of these bimbos who probably blew Mr. Ryder to get a part in this shit-sucking movie. Leave me alone! Let me go! I'm not done with that asshole. I want to see his teeth flying out of his mouth."

"You assaulted a man without justifiable cause."

"What are you, a lawyer as well as a cunt? God, and you're dating the troll. Figures you'd stick up for him."

"If you don't want charges pressed, you're going to calm yourself, and hear me out. That's all I ask. I promise what I have to say you need to hear."

"Yeah, whatever. I'm sure you're full of tips on how to do anal and deep throat without gagging."

"I've heard it all before, so keep it coming. None of it bothers me."

"Of course it doesn't. You're Candy Sweet. You're proud of being nasty you porno queen. Porno queen. Hah. What an oxymoron!"

Zoe couldn't resist Candy's hold anymore. She was out of breath, and so was Candy. The two stood together trying to regain the ability to talk. Candy was wiping sweat out of her eyes. She would have to redo her make-up.

Zoe was bright red in the face, and she kept huffing and growling, and getting more and more angry. The girl was about to have a panic attack. Candy got both of her hands on Zoe's shoulders and made eye contact with her.

"I only want to talk to you. That's all. You're all kinds of worked up. Breathe, okay? I don't want you to hyperventilate. Let's get you in the shade." She pressed her hand against Zoe's forehead. "Oh, you're burning up."

Candy guided her a few yards from the edge of the beach to a nice spot in the shade. "Breathe, okay? Breathe. Don't talk yet."

Zoe put her black hair in a ponytail aggressively and then bent forward to let the blood rush to her head.

"I'm going to get you some water, okay? I'll be right back, Zoe. Stay here. Promise me you won't go after Bruce."

Zoe nodded that she wouldn't.

Candy rushed to the canopy covering the table and grabbed a bottle of water from one of the many coolers. Zoe appeared to be much better when she returned. She handed her the water, and the distraught girl drank several gulps.

She put it out there for Zoe to understand. "You're going to stay sitting down and listen to me. I don't care if you like it. Hear me out. That's all I ask."

"Then say what you've got to say. No matter what, I'm going to rearrange that director's face. I'm going to punch his balls off. Then maybe he'll quit treating women like he treated Angie."

Something occurred to Candy. "Wait. I remember Angie Carmichael. I had a scene with her. We were both zoologists. We had two scenes together, actually. One was in a fake lab talking about the mutated dodo bird's corpse we were studying, and how a nefarious scientist was trying to bring extinct species of birds back to life, only he brought them back with insatiable hunger for human flesh."

"Aren't they always hungry for flesh?"

"That's beside the point. Let me finish. Our other scene together involved a ten minute filler of us lifting weights, doing aerobics, and stretching in the tightest spandex. Then we had a shower scene after our hard workout. We cleaned each other with the hugest sponge. I totally remember Angie."

"How's this supposed to make me feel better? Are you as dumb as you are a slut?"

She had heard much worse. It rolled right off of her shoulders. "You can call me all the names you want. I know what kind of work I've done. I'm a porno girl. I'm a cum dumpster. I've been banged every which way to Sunday. You can't do respectable Hollywood work once you've taken two dicks in the ass on camera."

"How can you talk like that? Don't you respect yourself?"

"When my boobs grew in, I always knew I'd make money off of my body. I wanted to be in movies, but I can't act worth a damn. I guess my breasts do the talking. You take advantage of your strengths."

"Wait, how did you get in the business anyway?"

"Like most girls do. I wanted to get away from my parents. My stepdad would get drunk and touch me. When I punched him in the throat and put him in the hospital, I emancipated myself. I stayed at friends' houses. When I wore out my welcome, I hitchhiked to wherever. I ended up in the San Fernando Valley. I was broke, hungry, and young. I answered a casting call for a model shoot.

"That model shoot turned out to be a porno. I did pretty good with it. The company turned me into Candy Sweet. I was what they call in the industry one of their "cover girls". I got swept up in it. I was using cocaine and boozing like crazy. I was headed in a bad direction.

"I hadn't worked with Bruce up to that point. He was making slasher movies at the time, but he hadn't had normal movie work in a while. He was going back into the adult business temporarily. That man saved me."

She had Zoe's attention. "How did that creep save you?"

Candy had tears in her eyes. Zoe held her hand. "I'm sorry. You don't have to tell me. Hey, I'm sorry for those things I said about you. I was pretty worked up. I was being a straight-up bitch."

"No, it's okay. I understand where you're coming from, honey. I do. Look, Bruce saved me from something horrible. I was in a porno involving a gangbang. Keep in mind, I'm super popular in the porno world. I'm the "it" girl. When you're the "it" girl, everybody wants to have a scene with you.

"Well, after this gangbang film, I shower, get dressed, and leave the studio which is really some dude's huge mansion. The guy who owns the mansion, he strikes up a conversation with me. He acts real nice, talks about how he let the director use his place for free, and like he's owed something. That debt is a roll in the hay with me.

"The man slaps me around, and he tries to get me to go along with giving him whatever sexual favors he wants. I can't get away or protect myself.

"Remember, the crew has left the house by now. Nobody is there but me and this psycho. But Bruce comes back. He left something behind. Bruce sees what's happening, and he takes a swing at the guy.

"He's so sweet. He can't fight worth a damn. This psycho beats the ever living shit out of Bruce. I'm talking broken ribs, broken nose, black eyes, and coughing up blood.

"Bruce tells me to run and call the police while he takes some serious punishment. The police show up and arrest the guy. Bruce goes to the hospital. He's a hero. The guy didn't really know me at the time, and he did what he could to protect me just because it was the right thing to do. That's how I got to know Bruce. That's how I fell in love with him."

"That's horrible what happened," was all Zoe could say. "So how come you still work in the industry?"

"I only work with Bruce. If he's making porn, I make porn. If he's shooting these animal attack films, I'm on board."

"I don't understand what this has to do with my sister?"

"It has everything to do with your sister. I have no respect for women who lie about being mistreated. After being attacked by that guy, I understand there are two sides to a story. Always.

"I remember the scenes I shot with your sister. She was more than willing to get naked and do softcore on camera. She signed a contract. Bruce discussed with her the exact details of the scenes. I was there when we auditioned Angie. If Angie told you Bruce made her do these things against her will, she lied to you.

"You don't like hearing that. I can tell by your face. I can show you the contract she signed and the details if you don't believe me."

Zoe's snarl didn't let up. "I'm not mad at you. I believe you, Candy. It makes sense now. When Angie came home, she was broke. Of course she'd tell a sob story to get my parents to let her stay with them and help her get back on her feet. She really played up her sob story. My dad was putty in her hands. When I see her again, I'm going to let her have it.

"I'm so stupid. I auditioned for a movie I didn't want to be in. I hung out with dumb drunk people on a boat for hours, and I did it all so I could punch out Bruce. God, I'm an idiot!"

Zoe was balling now.

Candy hugged her. "It's okay. Your heart was in the right place. You care about your sister. These things happen. It could be worse."

She was confused when Zoe's eyes were fixed to the sky. Her face went slack. She was chalk white.

"What is it?"

Zoe couldn't say it. She pointed a finger behind Candy at the sky.

She turned her head and froze. She saw it shuffling between several sets of high trees. The skyscraper tall body. The green and black plated skin. The bulging muscles. She could almost hear the muscles ripple with each stride. The yellow demonic eyes glowed with evil intentions. The teeth could chew a semi-truck into pieces. Candy wasn't a science wiz, nor was she an expert on dinosaurs, but there was no doubt that what she seeing with her own two eyes was a living, breathing T-Rex dinosaur.

The two women held tight onto one another until the beast moved on to another part of the island.

Zoe's eyes were trembling in the sockets. "We got to get on that boat and get out of here."

"Yeah, I'm with you."

They sprinted across the beach to warn the cast and crew of the threat lurking in the woods.

LESBIAN WATERFALL SCENE

Bruce was finding amazing locations on Pagoda Island. The local flora and fauna was unreal. He hadn't set foot on any Caribbean island before. There were stalks, and shoots, and odd blooming flowers the size of hubcaps. He was still stuck on the pink beehives dangling high from the palm trees and the orange banana trees. Everything was stunning and surreal and visually arresting, but he had to narrow it down to one location in order to get on with the show. This was a lesbian tits and ass scene. He didn't need to reinvent the wheel. The eyes wouldn't be on the neon blue flowers. They would be glued to the tits.

He selected the waterfall they stumbled upon on after walking through a half mile of strange forest. He chose a rock ledge platform with a waterfall threading against it. This was where his two nubile women would undress each other and make-out. The sun was shining down making the girls look like they were rising up from heaven.

"Okay, Bambi, you start kissing her neck. Then kiss her on the mouth. You don't have to tongue each other. Fake it. Be like lesbian mimes. Show your tongues in your mouth before you kiss, but you don't actually have to touch tongues. Tantalize us.

"Go ahead, and take off Beverly's top. Just pop it off. Yeah. Good. See. It popped right off. And Bambi, smile when she does that. Your breasts were suffocating, and now they're breathing. You're freeing each other from heavy sexual shackles. You are

35

romantically entangled, so stop looking like a baby that just filled her shorts.

"Yeah, that's good. Okay, start rubbing against each other. Grab her tush and squeeze it. Keep kissing, but you don't need to tongue. You're in love. You see unicorns, and rainbows, and an expensive engagement ring in each other's eyes.   Now let that water run over you and cool off your insatiable desires. Hear that sizzle.   You're scorching hot.   Inspire lesbians to be...well, lesbians. Lick her and smile. I like the way you're eying the camera, Bambi. You're fucking the audience with that babe gaze. You're giving the nation a hard-on. Yeah. Very good. Oh man, hot stuff. I'm talking jalapeno level heat. Now let's work our way up to ghost chili."

After the gratuitous making out scene, without tongue, Bruce asked Bambi and Beverly to swim across the water so their smooth backs and white globular buttocks showed above the surface. Just as rewarding to the viewer, he thought, would be the two re-dressing next to the waterfall to pad the movie time even further.

"Lovely scene, ladies. You two are naturals. Thank you so much for your effort. I know these scenes are nerve wracking. That's why we use only the absolutely necessary members of the crew out of respect. Thank you, thank you, and thank you. So inspiring, ladies. You've raised the bar. Truly."

Beverly and Bambi both said they were grateful for the acting opportunity.

They might not be so grateful when they watch this movie with their parents, Bruce thought with a smile.

"Blast, let's get back to the beach. We need one more filler shot. A good surfing scene would be nice. I saw some nice waves forming on our way here, so maybe we can take advantage of Mother nature. She's always free if she's agreeing with you."

Bruce and Blast gathered the shooting equipment.

Beverly and Bambi followed them back to the beach.

Where the two women had been swimming only minutes ago, Michael Rodman's head bobbed to the surface. The head floated across the bubbly blue water until a toad the size of a small dog with tiger stripes spotted the tasty treat. The tiger toad snatched the head with its pink taffy-like tongue from nine yards out. The creature swallowed it with three skull crunches and one hearty gulp.

DID YOU SEE THAT?

Blast asked the director, "What are you going to do about that Zoe chick? She's one dizzy bitch."

"What do you mean?"

"Well, she punched you in the face."

"What am I supposed to do? Put her in time out?"

"You know what I mean. She might become a problem for the shoot."

"Candy will get her in line. She can be persuasive."

"Yeah, you're probably right. But you never know with these millennial chicks. They think we're all here to serve their every need. Or they think they're a serious actor who should get the A-list treatment when they haven't earned the privilege."

"If Zoe is still a problem after Candy deals with her, she won't be in the movie. She can sit on the beach and read a book or hide in that boat until the three days are up. It's up to her. I'm not pushing anybody into anything. That's not my style. When I ask people to play my game, I always tell them the rules. Especially when it comes to our kind of movies."

"How's your nose?"

"Hurts. It stopped bleeding, though."

Blast stopped and gasped. He pointed to the left of where they stood. "Whoa! Did you see that?"

"See what?"

He pointed again. "*That*."

Bruce was searching through the thick of the woods. He didn't see anything moments ago, and he wasn't seeing anything now.

"I must've missed it. What do you think you saw?"

Blast scrutinized his surroundings. "I swear I saw it. Plain as day, Bruce."

"What was it? Just tell me. I've got a shooting schedule to complete here, buddy."

"I'm going to sound nuts. It was like a warthog, but it had eyes going down its entire body. I saw twenty eyes gawking back at me. Insane."

"That's crazy. Blast, are you staying hydrated?"

"Yeah. I think so."

"Come on. Let's get you some water. Just in case. I didn't see a damn thing out there."

SURF'S UP

They were back on the beach. Blast headed to the boat to grab a surfboard and a bottle of water to hydrate. Bruce went about picking the lucky hunk to ride the waves for the surf scene. The actors were standing where he told them to wait under a shady part of the beach.

"Okay, this question is for the guys. Any of you know how to surf? And be honest, please. I need you to surf for about five to ten minutes straight."

This was the moment of truth. If none of these guys raised their hands, he was going to have to get somebody who could fake surf. He pictured one of these morons bellyboarding waves for five minutes. The camera shots would be limited to make it more exciting than it actually was.

The silence didn't last long.

"I can surf, Mr. Ryder."

There was Rent Fulton standing there in his swim trunks. He was the only actor in the bunch who had graduated from film school and had performed Shakespearean theatre. He had blonde spiky hair, a six pack chiseled by the sharpest instrument, and a face that seemed to say "sure" to every suggestion.

Could this dude really surf? Then again, if this GQ guy couldn't and he tried to surf anyway, it would be equally entertaining to watch this straight-faced thespian attempt to hang ten. Bruce decided it was a win-win.

"Okay, Rent. You're our surfer guy. Why don't you warm up out there for a few minutes?"

"You got it, Mr. Ryder."

Blast returned with the yellow surf board. He handed it off to Rent. The actor rushed to the ocean as if his very paycheck depended on it.

"The rest of you actors," Bruce said, "need to stand and watch him ride the waves. Be shocked and awed at your friend who surpassed your expectations of his abilities. If you don't know how to react, then just keep saying "wow" under your breath and intermittently clap and jump up and down. That last part especially applies to the ladies. Okay, let's roll 'em."

Blast was staying on the outskirts of the crowd of actors keeping them excited and cheering by whispering suggestions to them. The director eagerly watched as Rent took to the water. At first, he was shaky and kept falling off his board. Once the kid got his confidence up, the actor was a regular pro. He slashed through the waters with zest. The idiot probably didn't realize it, but he had a giant moronic smile on his pretty mug.

Rent's going to look back on this as either the greatest time of his life or as something he'll pay to have erased from his record.

Either way, I'm in the money.

The camera guy was capturing Rent, and Blast was doing a fine job recording the audio of the friends cheering him on. Bruce's thoughts veered back to Zoe and the punch to his face. Candy and Zoe had been gone awhile. He hoped Candy had the situation buttoned up. After this scene, he would track them down if they hadn't returned.

A giant wave was fast approaching. Rent would get a piece of it. He thought to yell and warn the kid, but Rent saw it coming and gave everybody a big thumb's up. He was going to take surfing to a whole new level.

God, that grin. He looks like a damn oaf. I'll have to make that a screen shot on the back of the DVD release. That, and Beverly and Bambi under that waterfall. Smokin' hot stuff. I got a tent in my pants just thinking about it.

The wave had doubled in size in five quick seconds. Bruce wasn't so sure Rent knew what he was getting into. Blast was worried too.

"Hey boss, you thinking what I'm thinking?"

Before he could comment, Candy and Zoe were racing onto the set. They were waving their arms and screaming. He would've told them to be quiet, but the terror on their faces was so real.

"Everybody take five. What's wrong?"

Candy pointed at the other side of the island. "We saw it. I mean, it's out there. You won't believe it. The size. My God. We have to get on that boat, and get the hell out of here. We're all in danger."

Rent was poised on the board to dominate the ever-growing wave.

Bruce stared at where Candy and Zoe were pointing frantically. "Down that way. We saw it. A T-Rex."

He burst out laughing. "*What a relief!* I thought you guys were actually in danger. Great acting. I get your point. You two talked things out, and you discussed your scenes in the movie. I'll give you both more screen time even though you punched me in the face, missy."

Zoe grabbed Bruce's shirt by both hands. "Listen to us! This is no joke. We both saw a T-Rex in that forest. We were damn lucky it didn't spot us. It was stomping through the trees."

"I get it. You can stop now. You want more scenes. I'll give you all the screen time you want running around and being terrified. You sell it well, ladies. No problem. You've won me over with your budding talent. Now I've got a scene to finish. Please."

Rent had both arms out straight balancing himself. The top of the wave formed a ceiling over him. He was about to dip forward and dismount when everything came to a terrible halt.

PART TWO

TERROR BEACH

Candy clutched onto Bruce in horror. Zoe was screaming. Blast darted to his table to grab his 9mm. The cast and crew scattered. Some ran towards the boat. Others retreated into the forest. Bruce couldn't force his tongue to shape words. He would've demanded the actors to stay together and that he had the answer to fix this problem. All they had to do was regroup like with any other film that had suffered a major setback. But this wasn't any setback he was prepared to tackle. The director couldn't say a word because it was abundantly clear everything *wasn't* going to be okay.

Rent was acting like a super surfer. Everybody still on the beach was yelling at the actor to look behind him. He was oblivious to what rose up from the depths of the water.

The huge oblong reptile head had burst up from the ocean with rage and hunger in its eyes. The bass of its growl delivered tremors to everybody's feet and shook the trees. Waters sluiced, rippled, and boiled by the force of its immense form and strength. The ocean bent and broke to the monster's will.

When the T-Rex submerged, a wild ripple effect shot high tides of water onto the shoreline. The waters crashed and frothed towards the cast and crew. The motion obscured Bruce's ability to see Rent.

I have to save that kid.
It's my fault he's out there.

Bruce ran forward as fast as his body would allow. After only a matter of yards, he was already gasping for air and struggling to put one foot in front of the other. Candy was demanding him to come back to the shore. Don't be stupid. He couldn't save Rent. Bruce didn't listen. He was close enough that he could see through the wild splashing and surging of water to what was actually happening.

Rent finally caught sight of the T-Rex towering over him. The beast turned its eager-for-meat gaze down at the pretty boy. The monster released another ear-blasting growl. A split second later, the dinosaur snatched Rent off the surf board, and scooped him up into his mouth. Three bone crunching bites later, the inside of the dinosaur's mouth was colored with blood.

"You can't do anything for him you idiot!" Blast had the 9mm in one hand, and Bruce's arm in the other. T-Rex saw everybody on the beach and roared. The beast was only getting started. Rent was a mere appetizer to a lavish main course.

T-Rex shifted its body and lunged across the water towards the boat. That caused a sizeable wave to bash right into Blast and Bruce. Bruce was hoisted up five feet and then dropped. He landed face first against the sand. The shock of the blow left him momentarily paralyzed. He could only lay there and let his body absorb the shock of the impact. The way his head struck the ground, his hearing was muffled. Smaller waves were lapping up against him. He was soaked from top to bottom. Screams kept renewing themselves across the beach. That shriek and growl of the hideous beast would sound off every few moments.

The way his body felt, Bruce believed he could lay here forever. He thought every bone in his body was broken. He could move his hands and feet, but he couldn't get up.

Blood delivered him back up to his feet.

Rent's surf board washed up next to him. On that board were Rent's bloody feet up to the ankles.

"Oh God!"

Where's Candy?

You have to find Candy.

Bruce was shaky on his feet. He fell over twice before he could remain standing. He scoured the beach for his girlfriend.

Please, let her be safe.

She warned me.

This is my fault.

I should've believed her!

He saw a strange man across the beach at the very edge of the forest. He was a large linebacker sized man. He was dressed in dirty, ratty clothing. He had Candy over one shoulder and Zoe over the other. Both women appeared to be unconscious.

"*You son-of-a-bitch! What do you think you're doing? Stop!*"

The man paused, turned to regard Bruce with a "yeah, try and stop me" grin, and vanished into the cover of the trees.

Whoever the guy was, Bruce was going to deliver a beat down of the highest order. Nobody hurt his girlfriend. Nobody.

He raced over to the spot where the strange man had disappeared.

He only got half-way there.

T-Rex was standing over the boat. Bruce saw two of the cast members running into the below decks.

No.

That won't do you any good.

The monster saw you.

T-Rex raised its head back and whipped its tail. The boat gave to the dinosaur's strength. The tail smashed home. The ship imploded as if made of popsicle sticks. After the tail strike, the T-Rex dipped its head into the gaping wound of the deck and gobbled up the two actors. Every crick, snap, and pop echoed across the island including the final sickening *Gah-ulp* sound of it swallowing human meat.

The dino beast singled out Bruce. The monster stood knee deep in the water among the scattered and floating boat debris. The thing licked its chops and lunged right for the terror-stricken director.

THE CREEPY CASTAWAY

We're one in the same you and me. We're the last of our kind. No friends to play with. No family. Nobody to fuck. There's only meat to eat.

Nobody can understand us, because we're all alone.

We belong here.

This is our island.

Nobody will take it from us.

Nobody's going to leave here alive and tell the world about us. If a single one escapes, it's over for you and for me.

You and I are going to kill them all.

The strange man in a vest, undershirt, and cargo pants that had gone unwashed for months stayed on the outskirts of the attack zone. His big friend was keeping everybody else distracted. That allowed him to choose from the collection of frantic people.

I only want the best parts.

They're all so different, but their parts...their parts can make a perfect whole.

Look at these two fine pieces of meat. The butt meat. The tit meat. The between the legs meat. Individually, they're horrible, but together, they'll be so beautiful. It's been so long since I've had this fine a selection of pieces. And whatever I don't want...he'll take them. He's not picky in the least.

He clutched a hammer in one hand. He would have to move in real quick. Strike them hard, but not too hard. He needed them alive...for a time.

Candy and Zoe had watched T-Rex smash the boat into pieces. The noise would cover their screams, he thought.

Hurry, before he eats them all.

He vaulted out of the forest, slammed the hammer's head against the back of Zoe's skull. The conk sounded like a struck cue ball. Before Candy could see what had happened, he struck the hammer near the point of her skull. The blonde went down with one blow. Neither had time to utter a scream. He had hit many men and women unconscious with one blow. He knew how to stun and how to kill.

There's only one way to know if I hit them too hard.

They didn't fill their bikinis with shit or piss.

I think they'll be okay.

I have to hide them before they wake up. Then I can create a new friend. It's always nice to have company. It's been soooooooooo long since I've had good company.

He placed the hammer back into his belt loop made of dried out boar guts, hoisted each female over his shoulder, and disappeared into the forest.

WE HAVE TO SAVE THEM

Bruce closed his eyes. The T-Rex beast was seconds away from taking him in its mouth. He wouldn't save Candy. Whatever savage man the forest had spit out would have his way with her.

No.

I won't allow it.

I can't die like this.

He opened his eyes and stayed on all fours. T-Rex was yards from his position. He hadn't been eaten yet.

What the hell is it doing?

Blast was crouched nearby with his 9mm aimed at the dinosaur. He mouthed to Bruce, "Don't move an inch."

Bruce whispered back, "What? You going to shoot that thing? You need a fucking rocket launcher. That pea shooter won't do a damn bit of good."

The dinosaur was sniffing the beach. Each inhale and exhale seemed to punch the ground. T-Rex was chewing for thirty seconds before Bruce realized what was actually happening. Once he realized it, he dodged two fake severed heads and three legs. T-Rex spit each of them out, annoyed by the taste and the disappointment of not having actual flesh.

A series of shrill screams echoed from the forest. T-Rex was alerted. After studying the beach full of dead body parts for another moment, the dinosaur bounded through the trees to instigate more death and carnage.

Blast hurried to Bruce's side. "You okay? That thing didn't take a bite out of your ass?"

"No, I'm okay. Everybody else, I'm not so sure. Rent's dead. Some weirdo who looked like a castaway came out of the trees and grabbed Zoe and Candy. He took them somewhere, and I have to go and find them. He's going to do something awful to them; I can feel it."

Bruce struggled to get back to his feet. When he did, he was already moving towards the place he saw the man carry off the two women.

"Wait. Hold on. You can't just bound into the forest. That dinosaur is out there!"

"We're wasting time. The guy's going to kill them. Why else would he take off with them like that?"

"They're in trouble. Yes. We're all in big trouble here. Our boat's wrecked. The crew has scattered. We're in a shit storm of shit. I think we deserve half a minute to think."

"Give me your gun," Bruce insisted. "I'm getting them back."

"And what about the T-Rex? Can you navigate through the trees? If you haven't noticed, I don't think we're on the right island. Pagoda Island is a very well known island. I think if it had a living dinosaur on it, the world would've known it by now."

"What are you saying?"

"That idiot kid. The Rodman asshole. I think we're on the wrong island. Pagoda Island is populated in certain parts. This island doesn't seem to be. Again, if my logic serves me, they would've spotted the big ass T-Rex parading in the forest a long time ago. We're not where we're supposed to be. That kid took us to the wrong island."

"So what if you're right? It's all the same. I'm not standing here a moment longer. Candy's in danger."

"I'm saying let me help you. We need a few supplies. Just to be safe, I'll go with you. Two idiots are better than one."

Bruce couldn't stand the feeling welling up inside of him. He kept imagining the various ways a man could do harm to Candy. Just like Dalton Andrews who was the man that attacked Candy after that porn shoot. He vowed nobody would harm her ever again, and he would uphold that vow, T-Rex or not.

"Fine. Hurry."

"Now you're thinking straight. I'll only take one minute."

Bruce caught his breath and tried to get his head together. That would've been impossible if it weren't for the fact Candy was in danger. She was in danger anyway as long as that dinosaur was stalking them.

Before he could question how they were going to get off this island without a boat, Blast returned. He strapped on a backpack.

"I've got a flashlight, a few bottles of water, a first aid kit, and my 9mm. Let's go, mister director. I'll follow your lead. You saw them last."

Bruce did just that.

The two weren't very deep in the forest before they saw evidence of fresh carnage.

A MOMENT OF CONSCIOUSNESS

The rocks were the strangest colors. They were smooth on top as if something had sheared the tops off. She couldn't get over the colors, though. She remembered growing up and how her little brother collected comic book cards. He would make a big event out of tearing open each new pack, and when he found a hologram, watch out! The rocks were like a pool of 3-D colors. Like a holographic comic card. Every rainbow color appeared. Change your angle, and the color would change too. Watching them was hypnotic.

Candy focused on the rocks instead of the raging pain in her skull. A line of blood was drying down her face. Her head was foggy. She couldn't think straight. The rocks. The rocks were easy to interpret. Everything else, not so much.

As pretty as the long path of prism rocks were, she realized she was looking down upon them. She wasn't moving on her own. She was over somebody's shoulder.

She called out to whoever was carrying her. A soft moan crept from her lips. The person either ignored her or didn't hear her, because they didn't react.

They're saving me.

We were being attacked, I was hurt, and this man is saving me.

She was weak. Her eyes wouldn't stay open very much longer. Closing her eyes would be the easiest way to deal with the pain in her skull.

The rocks. The pretty rocks. She was saved. These were the things that mattered.

Candy slipped back into unconsciousness, but only right before seeing Zoe's face inches from her own, and how it was caked in so much blood.

The blood, coupled with the screams echoing from every pocket of the woods, told her she was anything but saved.

SHITTY WAY TO DIE

Logan Williams was the nineteen-year-old fresh-faced actor dressed in pink shorts with white polka dots. He was also the guy running for his life. Everybody else in the crew had fled the scene and went their separate ways. He ended up alone in the shuffle. He had torn up his aqua shoes against rocks the color of blue cotton candy. Across his back, something that looked like an owl with leathery wings and jowls like a foaming rabid dog had raked its talons deep into his skin. He kept moving despite the pain of the attack.

In this part of the forest, the trees were covered in a thick green moss. The moss was sharp as high grit sandpaper. He was bleeding from his palms when he made the mistake of bracing himself against one of the damn things.

One thing was clear.

Nature was quite the bitch on this island.

A green stalk reached out to grab him. The stalk was as thick as a human arm and triple as strong. Logan leapt forward to dodge the thing. The stalk opened like a sideways pea pod to reveal lance-sharp teeth. Logan gasped in horror when he got a closer look at the mossy tree the stalk was connected to. Along the surface, clear tubes were carrying chewed up arms, hands, skin, and guts. He saw Deborah Kingford's head in one of those tubes. The actresses' face was shaped in a forever scream.

Logan discovered an opening in the forest up ahead. He stepped across a path of smooth multi-colored rocks and was sprinting on flat open terrain.

Grass can't kill you, right?

He spun in place hearing loud blasts of agony and tortured screams. His friends and co-workers were dying out there.

He couldn't keep his eyes on one thing. The grass. The horizon of more forest surrounding him. The sun safe up in the sky. There were no buildings or signs of civilization. This was a wild island untouched by humans. There were no more rabid fucked up owls or hungry man-eating plants ready to attack him, and thank God. The way appeared to be clear.

Logan stopped one moment too late. He lost his footing. Underneath him, the ground was soft like mud. He struck the ground on his side. What he landed on squished. When he tried to get up, he used his hands to push off of the ground, and his hand sank deep and deeper into the muck that stank of many horrible things.

Wads of hair were twisted up in the dark gray mess. Bones of animals unidentified by science. White curvatures or ribs and backbones that could've been used to build ornamental harps. Eyes the size of softballs that were partially digested. Most of it was gray clay and soupy brown mud. The smell of it cut through his sinuses and induced vomiting.

This isn't mud.

This is shit!

I've fallen in T-Rex shit.

The realization seemed to make the pile deeper. He imagined a ten-ton elephant taking a dump. The pile was four feet high. He was sinking deeper and drowning. A dollop struck his mouth. He spat, and spat, and spat and vomited, and vomited, and vomited.

What he didn't expect hit him all at once and sucked every ounce of blood from his body in seconds. White maggots as long as garden snakes slid under his skin with the ease of hypodermic needles. Hundreds of intestinal parasites feasted on Logan's body until he was unrecognizable matter mixed in the giant T-Rex shit patty.

WEB AHEAD

"You're not taking him!"

Becky McAllister had hold of her new boyfriend, Fred whatever-his-last-name was-she-couldn't-remember, by both hands. T-Rex had Fred's well muscled body clutched in his mouth.

"Let him go!"

She pulled back as hard as she could and fell backwards with Fred's ripped off arms in her hands. Becky cried out as she saw armless Fred chomped up into T-Rex's mouth. The dinosaur seemed to smile at her horror. Those glowing yellow eyes were pure evil. She threw away Fred's arms and got herself together.

Becky had run track in high school. Her room's shelf was heaping with trophies. She used that athleticism and fled from the creature.

STOMP.

STOMP.

STOMP.

The ground quaked with T-Rex's pursuit. She leapt, jumped, and sped up her pace as she ran between the dense trees. That gave her the edge. T-Rex had to pummel and smash through them. She heard the beast head butt and smash its body through the trunks of trees. They were mere roadblocks to the sweet meat.

"*Ah-gawd!*"

Becky spat it from her lips and tried to peel the sticky spider web from her face. The web was so sticky, she stopped running so she could open her eyes again. The webbing was like glue. The mess was stuck to her fingers, but at least she could see again.

She would soon curse the gift of sight.

Someone kicked the feet from under her. She couldn't break her fall. She landed with a great whoosh of air escaping her lips. Her forehead was bleeding. The ground made rattling sounds. She thought it was porcelain, but it was actually broken up bones. They were scattered and piled inches high.

Becky was lifted up off the ground by her ankles. Her legs were pressed together. A wet thick rope was wrapped around both feet. That was what had knocked her on her ass. She was upside down and being carried upwards inch by inch.

She couldn't look up.

She could only look around.

Giant spiders the size of Mac trucks were climbing down the thicker trees. Their skittering was grating to her ears. These spiders were bone plated in the thorax. The rest of their body was covered in raw black glistening meat. She wasn't sure how they could see because they didn't appear to have eyes.

That question was answered when cords of pinkish leather fell from their bodies all around their circumference. At the tips of the leather cords, wads of meat opened up like eyelids. Green eyes with red speckles watched her. The fifty some odd morbid tarantula hybrids were surrounding her. Closing in for the kill.

The closest one had a mouth slit on its belly. Hundreds of teeth click-clacked together in anticipation of a juicy meal.

"*Raaaaaaaaaaaaaaaaaaatch!*"

T-Rex raised its giant foot and squashed the spider. Hot guts squirted from broken sections of its flesh.

The spiders combined forces and went on the offensive.

Becky was still being woven upwards.

She could only thrash and cry out.

Webs shot from every direction and attached themselves to the T-Rex. The dinosaur would chew through them or use that web as a lasso. Its small arms would swing the attached spider into a tree. The strength! The spiders slammed into the trees so hard they exploded into juicy bits. Another spider leapt onto T-Rex's back. T-Rex jumped up and landed back-first onto the ground. The wrestling move did the trick. Squash! The spider spurted bug guts from hundreds of broken orifices. The dinosaur quickly got up and chomped one of the spiders into nasty pulp.

The dinosaur was winning its battle.

Becky was not.

Winding upwards inch by inch, the smart spider perched up high up in the tree was reeling back in its web to bring her home. She could see the slit open in its belly, and those teeth, Jesus, those teeth...

TIGER TOAD

What just bit me?

Seriously. I don't feel so good all of the sudden.

There go my dreams of being a movie star. They would've loved me. All big time stars go through this. The humble beginnings. The slow climb up the ladder. Then finally the breakout film. It all would've started with Dino Buffet 3. *That's what that Rodman douche told me anyways.*

Oh man, I'm not feeling good at all.

John Anthony slid down the tree he was leaning on for support. The incredible dinosaur stalking them in the woods didn't matter anymore. The bite on his arm overarched everything else. He was tingling all over, and now he was numb. That numbness intensified into a paralysis. He was almost...high.

He imagined smoking the biggest bowl. This wasn't creeper weed, but good weed. The kind you didn't eat your weight in cheese doodles over. The weed the government had genetically enhanced for a superior high.

He was laughing and making a yucking noise.

It was really amusing if you looked at it the right way, John thought. What a funny looking thing to get bitten by. There it was crouched on a stone that served as an island in a large puddle of water. Calling it a toad wouldn't be doing it justice. The toad was orange with tiger stripes. Its head was sinking into its hulking fat body. The eyes were solid black. The thing had to be almost a hundred pounds. It was simply huge. Bigger than a dog.

How did it bite me?

Toads don't have teeth.

John turned his eyes down to his forearm. There was a wet sticky spot with a fat bead of blood.

Did the thing jab me with its tongue?

You've been poisoned by the tiger toad.

Tiger toad.

That would've been a cool name for a band.

Tiger toad.

The toad made a sharp chortling noise. The toad was like a balloon, somehow inflating itself from within, until it was three times its size. He thought the damn thing was going to pop. The toad was as big as a miniature pony now.

Before John could perceive anything else, the toad flicked its thick pink projectile tongue. The sticky end dug in like a spear deep into his bicep. The tongue retracted, and his arm was ripped right out of socket.

John watched in awe and confusion as he was leaking great amounts of blood.

Why was he laughing?

God, I'm so high!

I can't feel a thing.

This is great.

The toad flicked the tongue again and again and stole both of his feet. Flick. Flick. Flick. Now his other arm. The tongue shot into his belly and caught a hold of his guts. The intestines unraveled out the entry hole like a long pink piece of cooked spaghetti. It all went down the tiger toad's throat with a wild slurp.

I still can't feel anything.

Man, this toad injected me with some good stuff.

Wow, this is almost fun.

I'm sooooooo fucking high.

Mr. Toad, what piece you going to take next? My bet, you'll eat my ass cheeks. Gotta be the cheeks next.

He bet wrong.

The pink tongue fired out of the toad's mouth in three-dimensional fashion. The tongue poked out John's eye, plunging in deeply. The pink dagger dug into his brain and then quickly reared itself back. John's neck made a grump sound when his head was disconnected from the rest of his body. The tiger toad swallowed it whole. Minutes later, there wasn't a piece of John left to eat.

The tiger toad grew even bigger.

NOWHERE SAFE

"Ahh!"

The green, black, and blue beak pierced Jenny's left breast. *Peck-peck-peck-peck-peck.* The soft skin parted up against the razor-tipped weapon. Each connection was like a nail being driven into her body. Those beady buzzard eyes gobbled up a chunk of dangling breast meat and was about to delve its bloody beak right back into the wound.

Squawk squawk squawk!

Jenny Cole, Bikini Beachgoer #4, punched Toucan Sam from hell in the side, and then ripped out a handful of its rainbow feathers. The bird reared back its head and raged. The thing went for her eyes this time. Before it could take that killing lunge, another huge form swallowed the bird up in its mouth with strike speed. Every bone was crushed in the bird's body. The jaws compacted it into a bloody heap. The double-headed anaconda snake swallowed the bird whole. The giant snake's body was as red as the blood spilling from the bird.

"Ahh!"

Jenny back-pedaled on all fours from the threat. She pictured herself being crushed, devoured, and digested. She forced herself up onto her feet and fled in the opposite direction.

She made it four steps before crashing smack-faced into the leathery spider's leg.

"Ahh!"

Jenny dove away to escape being underneath the gargantuan spider and that hideous mouth. She landed hard on a flat patch of grass and froze.

Oh my God!

At the edge of the forest, the spider was pivoting its body to attack her. She imagined being real dead real fast. Then she heard it approach.

T-Rex leaped into the air and squashed the spider with both of its feet. The spider's guts spat out both of its sides with a broken fire hydrant's force. The spider collapsed deflated and dead.

"Ahh!"

T-Rex bounded after her. Its reptilian body was a sleek machine of speed. Pure hunter, pure hunger, pure energy, the dinosaur roared, announcing its dominance. Steps away from turning a vibrant, young woman with the rest of her life ahead of her into something to be excreted and returned to the earth, Jenny had nowhere to flee.

She closed her eyes, prayed for a quick merciful death, and was completely showered by mutant grasshoppers with thick shell bodies and sharp toothpick teeth. Before T-Rex could claim its kill, the jacked up grasshoppers had de-fleshed Jenny and left a pile of picked over bones.

"Raaaaaaaaaaaaaaaaaaaaaah!"

T-Rex stomped the colony of grasshoppers into the ground leaving a concave hole filled with tobacco juice blood.

The prehistoric beast, super pissed, returned to the hunt.

QUICKSAND TRAP

Gary O'Rear, Popular Kid #1, was moving his muscle bound body much faster than his co-stars. He had left them in his dust. Not that he felt bad about it. He wasn't being paid worth a damn to be in this movie. He didn't make any friends, really, while working either. And Bruce Ryder was a grease ball loser.

He was alive.

End of story.

Fuck the rest of them.

Besides, Gary was a real actor who had done commercial TV work and had jobs in a few supporting roles in real Hollywood movies. His pedigree didn't change things. The rent was due, and he needed that paycheck, and he was earning it, and now he was fighting for things more important than resurrecting his bank account from the dead.

He was somewhere in a fantastic forest. He imagined the rain forest was like something he saw as a kid in the movie *Ferngully*. Odd monkeys that were blue skinned and covered in green hair pointed at him and seemed to laugh at his situation. Trees with visible writhing veins and digestive cavities made his jaw drop again and again. Everything appeared to be a chunk of the prehistoric past as if the island had survived centuries of change and somehow remained the same.

Skip the nature tour.

How the fuck do I get out of here?

You can't. You saw the boat get smashed by that fucking dinosaur.

I'll build a raft. I don't care. I'm not dying here.

He was as stealthy as a running back racing for a touchdown until the ground unexpectedly dipped. He turned his ankle and was pitched forward. When he hit the ground, he splashed into a puddle. The puddle wasn't water. It was grainy and thick like oatmeal. The stuff was thick and heavy and sucked him right down.

Quicksand.

Gary cried out for help. The muck filled his mouth and left his pleas unheard. He spat it out in time to be dunked in the mess. He was lowering down deeper. Gary did his best to try and reach out and pull himself back to the top for that precious breath of air. The sand, the clay, the living dirt, whatever it was, weakened him against its power.

He wasn't going to survive this. He was close to blacking out when he fell and landed hard. Gary coughed for breath. Once he was breathing again, he took in his surroundings.

He was in what appeared to be a cave. He sweated in the humid environment. The ground and walls were slimy and smelled like that nasty smell of wet pavement and earthworms when they were forced up from their dirt hideaways after a good rain. Everything was a guess because he was walking in pure darkness without a hint of light.

Gelatinous goop was sloughing off the ceiling and landing in dollops against his head. The humidity level was increasing. Gary did the only thing he could and kept walking. The ground at his feet was hard to stand on. He imagined trying to keep himself upright while stepping on a waterbed. When he did slip and fall, it didn't injure him. He was grateful for that much.

The speck of light up ahead gave him the hope of escaping this quicksand purgatory cave place. He didn't know what to call it.

He'd give his left nut for a bar of soap and the right one for a shower. The light had him moving much faster. He was almost near the opening of this underground channel. The light was getting bigger and brighter.

Outside now, he could see details of the cave he had left behind. It wasn't a cave. His best guess, it was a port to a nest. The walls were a whitish blue clam color. Strange how the whitish blue suddenly stopped and the dirt began. This channel was made by a creature of some kind. Everything was covered in a thick sheen of a jelly-like substance. Gary, too, was covered from head to toe. If someone were to give him a hug, they'd slide right off of him.

I'm alive.

I survived quicksand.

If I get back to civilization, I'll have some kick ass stories to tell.

A rush of air coughed out of the end of the fleshy tube. The air increased, acting like a hard shove, and it pushed him to the ground.

The thing inside the channel was coming out. Gary caught some details of the worm face. The slit for a mouth. The sharp bone horn carved into a forward "V". The twenty-four beady black eyes locking onto him. The thing had to weigh many tons. The worm was incredibly long and thick in the body when it sprang from the hole. The worm didn't break pace to swallow him whole, then tunnel right back into the ground and out-of-sight.

HIDE AND SEEK

Regina Highwater knew there was strength in numbers. That's why she stayed with the chunk of the group that didn't scatter. She hid with twelve other members of the cast. They had made the right choice by staying out of sight. Staying put would save their lives.

She couldn't say what they were hiding under exactly. Crudely put, they were underneath a giant spinach leaf roof with a crispy texture. At their feet were shoots of random vegetation. The shadows underneath the leaf ceiling kept everything limited to a guess.

Whispers spread once the island went silent.

"You think it's safe?"

"How can I know?"

"How can any of us know?"

"The boat is gone. We're not getting off of this island."

"We'll find Bruce. He'll come up with a way of contacting help—there has to be a way."

"That idiot can't help us. If I find him, I'll kill him. What the hell did he get us into? The first chance I get, I'm calling my agent."

"Yeah, me too. I'm suing the bastard."

"I say we make a break for the beach. Maybe we can find enough pieces of the boat to make a raft. It might work. I was in Boy Scouts."

"Make a raft? Yeah fucking right. Nobody's going to do any of those things. We're not getting off of this island. You're forgetting about our giant green friend out there."

"We are going to make it. I'm not giving up on hope."

"Like hell we are!"

"Everybody be quiet. I can't hear."

Regina kept her ears trained. They were talking too loud. The last thing they needed was to draw attention to themselves.

"It's not going to do us any good being quiet. This island's full of monsters."

"This isn't Pagoda Island. Where are we then?"

"That idiot, what's his name? Mark Rodman. Yeah. That's right. Mark. He didn't know what the hell he was doing. If you guys weren't too drunk to notice, Mark looked scared the whole time he was at the wheel."

"Oh yeah? Then why didn't you do anything about it?"

"I didn't know. I wasn't sure. Even if he did take us to the wrong place, I never thought it would turn out to be anything like this."

"And now we're fucked."

"I never should've signed on for this third-rate crap."

"I'm never going to see my family again. They'll never know what happened to me."

"*Shhhhhh!*"

Am I the only one that doesn't want to get eaten?

Regina didn't hear the noise. She felt it.   This wasn't the sonic boom of a giant's steps. Those were soft, slow, and creeping. The sound that disturbed her was the strange sniffing. She couldn't see beyond the spinach leaf ceiling to view the source. Regina didn't need to see it, because she knew what was smelling them out.

The sniffing stopped yards from their hideaway. Everybody was stock still and holding their breath.

The silence gripped them all in terror.

Had they been discovered?

Was the dinosaur about to move on somewhere else or go in for the kill?

A rush of air careened against them. The spinach barrier was lifted up like a stiff tarp and blown away. They were the insects revealed beneath the rotting log. Everybody froze. Others ducked. Many cried. Regina heard prayers to God. One of her co-stars flipped T-Rex off and unleashed a colorful tide of insults.

Regina did what many did and cried for her life. T-Rex bent down and scooped them up in one big bite. The giant tongue, the dark colorful flesh walls of its mouth, the solid-as-bone roof of its mouth, everything blurred as if she were in a washing machine's spin cycle. She watched teeth crunch down and cut people in half, split people long ways, and dismember them. The mouth closed completely.

Darkness engulfed them.

She couldn't think with all the events taking place. The enormous tongue threw Regina upwards. She struck the ceiling. She was dazed but still conscious. If nature was merciful, she would've died then.

The mouth had turned into a mosh pit as the tongue swished them around. A tide of mouth juices covered them in a pool of burning acid. Everybody was turned into boiling blood and bone soup by the time T-Rex swallowed them all.

THE MISSION

The chewed up torso with a blue bikini top was Michelle Kelly. The arm torn from the shoulder with the Jesus fish tattoo on the bicep was Vick Lumley's. The single breast left with deep nibble marks—well, Bruce thought, that could've been anybody from his cast. The pieces of victims were scattered everywhere.

Bruce couldn't avoid that sinking feeling.

He didn't know how to find Candy and Zoe.

Blast was getting impatient with the search. "Where the hell are we going, Bruce? Face it. We're clueless as to the direction that guy went with our girls."

The forest seemed to spin fast on an axis. The trees got taller, and denser, and impossible to take in with the naked eye. Bruce was too angry to give up and too realistic for false hope.

"Look, man, if a big helicopter arrived to pick us up, I wouldn't leave without Candy or anybody else who might be alive. I owe them that much. This was my movie. This wouldn't have happened if I hadn't arranged for us to be here."

"It's not your fault on that account," Blast argued. "That idiot Rodman kid took us to the wrong island. It's clear this isn't Pagoda Island. Pagoda Island is inhabited. This place is overrun by monsters."

"Yeah. We can't forget we're still in danger ourselves."

The *Dino Buffet* movie was cancelled, but the buffet itself was not. The wild spatters of blood randomly spread out on the ground proved that much.

Get it together.

Focus.

How do you find someone you're looking for?

Of course! You find their tracks.

He shared the idea with Blast. Blast wasn't pleased with the suggestion, but he scanned the mossy ground for indentations anyway. They had nothing else to go on except for blood and fear.

They scoured for half a mile, trudging through thick bamboo patches, stomping on a hill of fallen boulders a strange fuchsia color, and stopping at what looked like a man made pathway. The stones were bizarre. The surface was smooth and multicolored. They reminded him of prisms.

"Bruce, you see these?" The special effects guy pointed at a pair of foot prints. "You ask me, these don't belong to anybody on our crew. They're from heavy duty boots. Everybody here is either wearing sneakers, sandals, or going it barefoot. Assuming this island is unpopulated by people, best bet, this is from our guy."

"Look. He stepped onto the path. I can see blood drops." Bruce bent down to touch them. "They're not dry. These are fresh. If he's done something to them—"

"We'll pay him back in spades. I'll make sure of it. Who do you think this guy is anyway?"

"Some castaway creep. Who knows?"

Blast clutched onto his 9mm that much tighter. "Figuring he's survived on this island, he's got a few tricks up his sleeve. He knows the terrain and the places to hide."

"Why hide here at all?"

"Maybe he's running from something. Or he's a crazy miserable castaway, like you said. God knows what's up with this fucker."

The roar in the sky gripped them both. They could see the T-Rex's shape from afar. The mega reptile had its head tilted back. It opened its mouth and chewed down hard. Blood from all sides of its mouth gushed forth. Bruce imagined mowing down on a burger smothered in way too much ketchup. Blood and human pieces erupted from the sides of his mouth.

"Get down," Blast said. "Stay low. Be quiet."

Bruce had no problem obeying the commands.

They listened to the chomping and groaning of hunger satiated and created in the same breath. Bruce shivered picturing himself being eaten.

This beast's appetite is bottomless.

How many people were in its mouth?

The T-Rex was gone. It bounded after the next prey. How many members were left in his crew by now?

"Bruce, my God, are you seeing this?"

The sight up ahead was very morbid.

A BAD SIGN

The path of prism stones abruptly ended. Bruce could only describe what was up ahead as a sacrificial or ceremonial circle. Animal skulls and bones lined that circle. These skulls were made of antelope, gorilla, boar, pig, and skulls that could've passed for cavemen skulls. At the center of the circle was a steel pole jammed into the ground. There were chains and shackles attached to the pole. He knelt down on the dirt and saw more of the blood drops. The guy had crossed through here recently.

"We're on the right track. Keep following the blood."

Blast was fixated on the steel pole and the skulls. "I don't get it. This guy arranged the animal skulls. He set up this pole and the shackles."

"Yeah. So what? Let's get moving. The guy's fucked up. Easily established."

"But why is he sacrificing people here? How did he get people to sacrifice in the first place? People don't come here. So how did they get here?"

"Maybe these people were like us. They happened upon the island on accident."

"Yeah, but with the number of human bones here, it's impossible. This guy has to be leaving the island and coming back. He must bring people here to sacrifice."

Bruce was hit by the implications of the question. "Why would he do that? If he's not a castaway, and he can leave the island, why come back at all?"

Blast's face was locked in worry. "This guy's got something super fucking weird going on here."

"Then let's hurry up and find this guy."

The concerns had them moving much faster now despite the heat and humidity. The sun was bearing down on them hard. They took turns drinking from a bottle of water.

The blood drop trail took them near a sizeable lake. There was a wild boiling in the blue waters. Bruce imagined something huge rising up from the depths.

Director and special effects man both hurried away from the lake. After the lake, the blood drops seemed to stop completely. They faced a wide open valley of grass with no trees or vegetation. Across the way, there was a large hill. On top of that hill was a two-story mansion.

"That has to be where the guy took them," Bruce said. "Come on, let's go."

Once they stepped into the open valley, things came at them from all angles. It sounded like a roaring stampede was coming right for them. A wall of dust obscured what was drawing nearer. This was easily the most danger they've been in thus far, Bruce thought, and it wasn't going to get any better from here on out.

SEPARATED

Bruce didn't know where Blast went. The special effects guy's shape was engulfed in the flying dust wall. Sounds of grunting, squealing, and animal cries of panic circled him. He caught fifty boars with giant tusks and eyes covering their bodies from top to bottom book it in the opposite direction. Zebras, antelope, and deer with taller legs, thicker bodies, bulging muscles, and rainbow stripes were racing to safety. The sight would've been amazing if it wasn't so alarming.

"Run, Bruce! Get to the hill. Save the girls!"

That was Blast's voice. Bruce still couldn't locate him.

The 9mm barked. The shots echoed from everywhere. Bruce called out to his friend, and he didn't answer. If the man did, the stomping of hundreds of hooves covered his words up.

STOMP.

STOMP.

STOMP.

T-Rex was charging. Its mouth was slightly open. Drool edged down its face looking like rubber glue mixed with diseases and old blood. The dinosaur was about to lunge forward and swipe at the weakest row of animals running for their lives when out of the dust came something just as big as T-Rex and ten times as wild.

The creature was squat, and its surface area was huge. This thing weighed many tons. Its skin was bumpy with ridges that were sharp as bone. The colors along its body were magnificent.

The orange, black, and white of tiger stripes and the body of a toad.

It used its back legs—those taught, tight, and ripped powerful muscles interlaced with even more muscles—to butt its head into the side of T-Rex. T-Rex didn't see the opponent coming. The tiger toad's head struck with earth shaking impact.

With a roar of pain, T-Rex went head over heels onto his back. Tiger toad stayed in place, all four legs bunched up against its body. The toad opened its mouth. The act was the unhinging of a great drawbridge. Skin stretched, and stretched, and stretched. The sound grated against Bruce's ears. The toad's belly expanded in anticipation of filling it.

The pink tongue blasted out of its mouth. He imagined a machine gun spitting out bullets, how the tongue flick, flick, flick, flick, flicked in rapid succession. Each lashing touched onto a boar, an antelope, a buffalo, and more, and more, and more. The toad dragged them all into its mouth. Each animal was swallowed whole. Twenty seconds were spent eating when the toad closed its mouth and hopped away.

When T-Rex rose back up from the attack, the other animals were long gone. T-Rex was alone. The king of the island, now dethroned, threw its head back and roared with fiery anger. It stomped the ground, kicked at the dirt, and kept roaring and screeching.

Bruce didn't wait for the dinosaur to see him standing there like a big idiot. He searched for Blast. There was no way to know where he had gone or if he had survived. He ran towards the hill, made it across the long front yard, and located a back door at the mansion. He prayed this was where he would find Candy and Zoe.

REX RAGE

The dust from the stampede had settled, and T-Rex trudged towards the shelter of the forest. One side of his ribs were crushed. He had to recoup, strategize, and come back one hundred percent before going on with the hunt, because the hunt had changed.

It wasn't the pain that enraged him, nor was it the hunger, or the denial of a good meal.

This was his island. He was king. He inspired fear. He dominated. He was the last of his kind, and he knew it. Before going completely extinct, he wanted to live out his final years enjoying complete dominance.

But now, he was being challenged by an adversary he hadn't encountered before. The primal inner workings of the dinosaur's brain imagined hundreds of ways he could tear the tiger toad into bloody ribbons.

First, he had to recover. He crouched down low, closed his eyes, and slept. For when he awoke, he would be a new beast. Everything in sight was going to die. Every piece of meat and drop of blood would cross his teeth and wet his palate.

The tiger toad would perish by his will.

T-Rex vowed it as the primordial jellies in his brain boiled for revenge.

T-Rex dreamed of death and feeding.

When he woke up later, no life on the island would be left unsettled.

TOAD DREAMS

Tiger toad burrowed itself in the soft cool mud located around the nearby sizeable body of water. It wasn't injured nor was its pride damaged by the short-lived battle. Even conquering the king of the island wasn't on its mind. The magnificent toad only wanted to digest its food and eat some more.

The toad closed its eyes. The creature could feel animals being melted down in its acid pit for a belly. Hooves and animal cries beat against the walls of his stomach only to be reduced to liquid moments later.

Like the T-Rex, this toad was the only one of its kind. A misfire out of a toad's womb. Something that was meant to be aborted by nature had somehow survived and was rapidly growing. Nature couldn't contain this toad's insatiable instincts. Eat, and eat, and eat, and grow, and grow, and grow.

The toad was now a ten ton force. There were no limits to how huge it could become nor any limit to its hunger. Even full to the point it could burst, the tiger toad imagined its next meal. The crunch of bones. The way it felt to stick and wrap his tongue around a fighting, crying prey.

There was one item on the menu the toad especially craved. This required every vacant inch of his stomach. He would burrow in the mud for weeks after eating this grand meal.

The tiger toad slept and dreamed of how magnificent it would be to eat T-Rex.

GORY SIGHTS

Candy opened her eyes and fought through the fogginess of being knocked unconscious. She didn't expect to wake up in a room. The first instinct was to believe she was back home. She was saved. Everything was going to be okay. Nothing was going to eat her. The one thing that kept her from believing that was the wretched smell. Something in this house was rotting, and she stifled her need to wretch against the stink.

When she tried to move, she realized she was strapped to a steel gurney. Zoe was beside her in another gurney. The girl was unconscious. Candy envied the girl. She was still a child safe in her dreams and not awake in this nightmare reality.

This wasn't a single room. This was the entire top story of a big house. The walls looked to have been knocked down by a sledgehammer. It was easy to deduce why the walls were knocked out. Every inch of space was used. Strange things were propped in corners and held up in proud displays.

A collection of hideous collages.

God, the smell, she kept thinking. *I'm going to choke on the smell.*

The windows had no curtains. Sunlight bled into the long and wide room. Everything was illuminated with perfect lighting. There were no shadows to mercifully conceal what occupied the area with her.

Her eyes studied the sights and tried to dissect them and understand them. Blackened skin. Dried up husks for bodies.

Blue-black flesh. Yellow-purple bruised skin. Every shade of death and decay, these collages featured them in every color.

Sharpened poles were jammed through human torsos to prop them in standing positions. Another sharpened pole was jammed crossways so severed arms and legs could create a rough cut of a human body. Male and female arms and legs and heads were used at random.

The facial features of this fucked up corpse art was the worst thing to behold. Livers and spleens were jammed into mouths to make cheeks puffy. Eyes were hollowed out so long intestines could dangle from them. Exposed brains served as glue to keep scalped heads of hair stuck in place. Hands were cut off and hearts were put in their place. Candy counted fifteen bodies mutilated, cut up, and crudely put together like some third grader's craft project.

The drip, drip, drip caused her eyes to dart to the corpse sculpture on the left and over three collages. This was the freshet display. Red was oozing from the combined bodies in thin rivers. She could see swimming trunks on the pelvis, female legs from the knees down, and lungs for feet. The face looked like two skulls were smashed together and somehow stayed melded together. The yin yang of two female heads wore expressions locked in terror screams. Out their brains, two severed hands reached out as if extended for help. She recognized the faces of the actors. The way the pieces were partially devoured, she believed this guy had picked up the pieces T-Rex has discarded from today's attack.

Candy was weeping. That would be her soon. She would be carved up and put on some butcher block's display. The life she lived, her experiences, her future, they would all add up to gore on some fucked up psychopath's canvas.

She fought the thick leather straps that held her down. The gurney's rusted wheels shifted back and forth in protest. The only thing she was accomplishing was making a bunch of noise. She had so little energy, and what she was doing was futile anyway. She was strapped in nice and tight and helpless.

Candy sucked in a breath and did the only thing she could think to do, and that was SCREAM.

Her screams were answered by footsteps rushing up the stairway from the first floor.

Soon she would meet her captor.

SNEAKING AROUND

Bruce had to be quiet. He wanted to sneak up on the son-of-a-bitch who had taken the woman he loved. He wasn't a strong man. He couldn't fight, but the feelings that had been building up inside of him the past few hours encouraged him to believe otherwise.

When he opened that back door to the mysterious house and closed it behind him, he was no longer emboldened. He was dropped right back into a fearful state.

My God, what is this son-of-a-bitch doing here?

This was just like many of the cheap slasher movies he made in the '80's. But this was the genuine article. He thought psycho killers and demented weirdoes were a thing of pure imagination.

The basement was pitch black. The only source of light was from an open door coming from the top of a wooden stairway. The light offered enough illumination for him to see the outlines of what lay on the ground. Piles of bloody clothing were left in a giant heap. Shirts, shoes, dresses, purses, jewelry, bras, and panties by the dozens had been discarded and left there. A smell added to what he was viewing. It was easy to deduce the reek. They were rotting bodies. In this heat, a putrid humidity filled the house. He covered his mouth with his hands to stifle the urge to vomit. He couldn't afford to be heard. He needed the jump on this guy to save Candy.

One thing was for certain now.

This was where the castaway creep lived.

Bruce edged his way across the basement. He listened. He didn't hear anything. Then he froze. He heard Candy unleash a terrorized scream. A man upstairs suffered a fit of phlegm induced coughing. He spat something out onto the floor, grunted, cleared his throat, and his feet touched the floor.

"It's about time one of those bitches woke up," he muttered to himself. "They're about ready."

They're alive.

Thank you, God.

He was headed in the direction of the stairs when something stirred in the basement from the corner.

Bruce realized he wasn't alone.

CASTAWAY CREEP

Candy couldn't believe her eyes. The man was hideous. Only his cheeks, eyes, and forehead were visible. The rest of his face was covered in a long, bushy, gray beard that looked to have been dipped in oil. His skin was a flaking sunburned red. He had a deviant's scowl. His eyes studied the length of her body..

Her eyes weren't focused on his tattered clothing or that peculiar tang of piss emanating from him, but instead, she focused on the cloth bundle in his hands.

He spread out the cloth along the floor. Inside, metal clanged together. He played his dirty, grit caked hands along the collection of instruments. There were five different sizes of scalpels. Hammers of various types: mallet, ball peen, and carpenter's. A small hatchet. The thickest meat cleaver she'd ever seen, and her dad was a deli butcher.

"Stay," was all he said to Candy, before getting up, going downstairs, and then shortly returning. He had an armful of steel poles. He placed them near the cutting tools.

Candy gave a short snort when he moved to Zoe. She was still unconscious. The rise and fall of her chest indicated she was alive.

The man trailed his hands along her jaw line. He played with her hair, spreading out the dark strands. He trailed his finger down her lips.

"It gets awful lonely on this island sometimes," was all he said, breathy.

He pressed on her abdomen like a doctor would during an examination. Then he slipped his hands underneath her bikini and cupped her full breasts. He gave a shudder.

When he tweaked her nipples with his dirty fingers, Zoe's shock filled eyes sprang open. She screamed, but not before throwing her head forward and head butting him.

The man didn't expect the blow. He tripped over himself, falling backwards.

"Candy!" Zoe turned to her. "Did he hurt you? Tell me you're okay."

"Yes. I'm okay. For now, I guess."

Zoe's face lost all color. She smelled the horrible reek of death. The sight of bodies on display in such bizarre fashion made her cringe in horror.

"What should we do with them, Mother?" The man had returned to his feet. He was talking to a corpse with a head of silver curly hair. This corpse was more like mummified remains. She wore a house dress and wore leathery, sunken skin. "Should we carve her up into a good little girl, huh, Mommy?"

The man spoke like a ventriloquist, talking from the corner of his mouth. He mimicked the voice of a crotchety old lady. "*Good girls don't know when they see good boys. Bad girls don't want to be good. They want to be bad. They're trash. Sluts. Whores. Harlots. They use their female parts for evil. They know men are weak. Like you, boy.*

"*But I'm a Christian woman. I believe there's good in everybody. Even the whores and sluts can be redeemed. You must separate the good from the bad and rebuild these harlots. Cut the flesh and remove the evil. That's the only way to save these nasty girls.*

"*I think you've found the right women this time. These other sculptures came close. It wasn't your fault they turned out bad. They didn't have the right parts. You tried, Timmy, you really did try, God bless your big ol' heart. You deserve the best woman. The perfect girl. That's why I tell you to keep trying. These two women you found can make one good girl. Then you can finally settle down and have children. The rest of these attempts you don't need anymore. Get them out of here. They're ripe. They stink! We don't need their company anymore. Throw them out that window over there."*

The man spoke with his normal voice. "Of course, Mother. You're right."

He opened up the window behind Candy and Zoe. The two girls didn't move or talk or breathe. What was happening was too unbelievable. No sane human being could react to this situation, Candy thought.

She prayed for many things in the coming moments. She prayed for Bruce to save her. She prayed for escape off of this island. She prayed they could save the lives of their fellow crew members. Most of all, she prayed to get the fuck away from this Goddamn psycho.

One by one, the man picked up the fetid sculptures of gore. The man was crying as he was pitching them out the window. Pieces of them would slough off the metal bars and splat onto the wood floor. The smell was horrible before, but now bellies were broken, intestinal cavities torn open, and all the gases, bacteria, and juices played on the air. Colonies of maggots, and even the occasional rat, were uncovered during the transfer.

The strange man was sobbing to himself. "I'm sorry, Brian. You're my best friend. But Mother says you have to go. She knows best. What Mother says goes."

He lugged a head sinking into a pile of wet guts and slopped it out the window. The man kept going back between himself and his Mother's voice between pick up and drop-offs.

"I'm sorry! I care about all of you so much. I love you with all of my heart. Forgive me!"

"*You're a big boy, Timmy. You know you're doing the right thing. Now quit being a sniveling brat.*"

"Yes, Mother! They're only my best friends. I'll stop being a human being. I'll repress my emotions, Mother. Yes, Mother! Anything you tell me to do, I'll do it!"

"*Boy, never talk to your Mother like that. I brought into this world, and I can take you out of it.*"

He was now clutching onto two fetid breasts sinking into the gnarled bones of a sternum. "Not her, Mother. Please. She's different. I really liked Beverly. She gave me the sweetest kisses."

"*I bet that whore gave you the sweetest kisses. I caught you sticking your little thing in that pile of mess. The awful grin on your face. You defied me. My Timmy. The boy I raised. I didn't raise no boy to act like that towards a lady.*"

"Fine. You're right. She's gone. She's out of this house. You happy? Huh? You pleased, Mother?"

"*I'll be happy when you speak to me with respect.*"

"Forgive me, Mother. This isn't easy. I'm sorry. I didn't mean to snap at you."

"*You care about people. You only want to see the best in each and everybody. That's what you're good at. You show off the best in them. It's such a wonderful thing what your father taught you. People viewed him as a meager taxidermist. Nobody realized he was a visionary. God gave him the eyes to see the good in people. God gave him the hands to cut out the evil and to display the good. This is preservation of humanity. God gave you the same abilities, son. Preservation. Goodness. The gift of seeing.*

"*I always wanted you to create a woman you could love. A good woman. You take these two women, and you make something spectacular with them. When you do that, you can finally enjoy the pleasures of a woman. You can kiss her all you want. Wouldn't that make you happy?*"

"Oh yes. Very happy, Mother. Very, very happy."

Candy heard this and kept seeing gore and sloppy pieces being dropped out of the window. The sounds. The smells. The dripping. She couldn't take it any longer. Screams ripped out of her throat. Zoe joined her. They were both pleading out for help.

"Silence them, Timmy! They'll upset the creatures outside."

"Yes, Mother."

The man picked up one of the scalpels and placed it up against Candy's throat. He brought his wet lips up next to her ear. Timmy made a wet slurping noise to clear his mouth of heavy saliva. Every breath he expelled stank.

"You two keep screaming, those monsters out there will come in and tear us to pieces. I keep them at bay by going back to the mainland and bringing T-Rex his sacrifice. I honor the king of the island, and they let me live among them in peace in exchange. Do you want me to tie you up out there for him to find and eat you later? I can look for more women with nice tits and pretty skin. You're not the only one pretty out there."

Candy shook her head, that no, she didn't want to be eaten by anything. Yes, she'd be quiet. Zoe promised the same.

"You two should be honored. I'm going to bring out the best in you and combine your bodies into something truly beautiful. Who wants to go first?"

"Go fuck yourself you Goddamn psycho!"

Bruce lunged at the man. He swung hard, throwing his whole body into the blow. His fist plowed into the man's jaw. Timmy fell over Zoe, rolled across her body, and struck the ground hard.

The director was about to go in for another punch. Timmy was too fast. He was right back up on his feet with a hammer in his hands. The man swung it with a killer's determination. The hammer struck Bruce on the shoulder, then the chest, and then the side of his eye. Caught up in a whirlwind of pain, Bruce couldn't defend himself.

He fell to his knees with blood streaming down his face. Timmy towered over him and raised the hammer high to drive home a death blow.

FIGHT FOR YOUR LIFE

Bruce was slow working his way up the stairs. Then he heard Candy and Zoe scream. He had no reason to be stealthy or quiet anymore. He lunged into the room. The sight of the man up close was a shock. He imagined a bum who'd dipped themselves in river water, piss, and took a shower in shit. Bruce didn't hesitate to challenge the man who literally reeked of the word "killer". The first punch landed so hard, his own fist flared up in pain.

He didn't care. This man had tied down these women to gurneys with instruments spread on the ground. God knows what he was really up to here.

Before he could do anything else, he spun to his side. He was struck three times. Hot sticky blood filled his eye. Before he could shake off the blows and get back to his feet, the castaway creep raised his hammer. He was a split second from bringing it home over his skull.

Candy was calling out to him to watch out, snap out of it, and for God's sake, dodge the attack. Zoe's words were indistinguishable shrills.

"You're not touching my friends ever again!"

Three booming shots resounded. The castaway creep was thrown backwards, smashed through the window, and fell from the second story down into the front yard.

Blast stood there with the 9mm extended for a few seconds before getting over the shock that he had gunned a man down.

"Is everybody okay?"

He helped Bruce up to his feet. Bruce rushed to the gurneys, undid the leather straps, and freed the girls. Candy hugged Bruce, and Zoe hugged Blast.

Candy said, "Thank God for you."

"Yeah, Blast," Bruce agreed. "You saved my ass. You're the hero."

When the room went silent as they heard steps coming up the stairs. Everybody was worried except for Bruce.

"It's okay." He moved towards the entrance of the room. "I found another person downstairs. This guy kidnapped her. Her name's Kate."

Kate stepped up to the group hesitantly. She could've been between eighteen and twenty years old with a short auburn bob haircut. She was a lithe one hundred pounds. Her summer dress was dirty with blood and dirt.

Candy smiled at her. "You poor thing. How did you get here?"

Kate had a small, meek voice. Terror underscored every syllable. Bruce listened to her, and knew she would be scarred for life.

"He took me. I was on the beach with my friends. That weirdo attacked us with a hammer. He killed the other two the night he brought us to the island. He hacked Nora up in this room. I had to listen to her screams. They lasted for hours. And Debra, he fed her to that dinosaur."

"You don't have to talk about if you don't want to," Zoe said. "It's over. The guy's dead. And thank God he is."

Kate saw the mummified remains of Timmy's Mother. She couldn't stand it. She grabbed the corpse by the arms and heaved her out the window. "Stupid bitch!"

She moved away from the window and unleashed her pent up horror.

"I've been here for two days. All I hear is that guy talk to himself. I can't get his voice out of my head. I learned plenty overhearing the bastard talk to himself. Chatty psycho, that guy. I'm studying criminology. I've read a lot of true crime. I know all about this creep. The guy's name is Timmy Blunt. His father was Darrel Blunt. Darrel was a professional taxidermist and a religious head case to boot.

"He would do his thing with animals during the workday, and at night he would find people he deemed immoral, cut their so-called good parts out, preserve them in jars, and leave the bad behind. Darrel got to the point he was stitching, grafting, and making new people out of these parts. You saw Timmy's work earlier. His father was along the same lines.

"Darrel's wife, Mildred, would help her husband differentiate the good pieces from the bad. Timmy watched everything as a child and learned the nut bag craft. He earned the nickname Taxidermy Tim. I guess the police were onto Darrel, so the three got onto a boat and escaped to this island. They were able to build this house and everything. Don't ask me how. I guess the psychopath family got creative."

"What about T-Rex and the messed up monsters out there?" Bruce asked. "Wouldn't that keep them busy?"

"If I heard Timmy right, he said the island wasn't full of these things until a large body of water separating one half of the island from the other dried up. When it dried up, the whole island was taken over by the creatures from the other side including that T-Rex. Timmy survived the change, but his parents did not. His Mother was bitten by a poisonous moth, and Darrel was eaten whole by the T-Rex.

"I don't know how long Taxidermy Tim has lived on this island or how he avoided being killed for this long."

"The taxidermy douche is dead," Blast said. "And thank God that's the end of that story. It looks like he was going back and forth between the island and America to kidnap new victims."

"Did I hear you right, Kate?" Bruce asked. "You saying there's a boat on this island?"

Kate was regaining her natural voice. It was now edgy and full of bite. "Taxidermy Tim talked about a path down from this house. It forks two ways. He said one side of the fork leads to the boat, and the other fork leads to death."

Bruce threw up his hands in resignation. "Jesus, are you kidding me?"

"How can we trust a psycho like that?" Candy posed. "He tried to cut us up to make a fucked up sculpture with our pieces. Keep in mind, you got all of this information while the creep was babbling to himself."

"What else do we have to go on?" Blast posed. "We're marooned otherwise. We could build a raft, but by the time we build it, we'd be attacked by whatever's out there. We need something to jump right on and get going fast."

Bruce looked on at the four other people and knew they had a shot to survive. It wouldn't be easy, but it was a shot, and they had to take it.

"Here's the plan. We find whatever weapons we can in the house, stick together, locate that path, and take our chances. It's all we got. We need to do this before sundown. Once it gets dark, forget it."

The group didn't waste time.

They scoured the house for weapons.

NOT DEAD YET

The bullets had gone through him cleanly.

No major organs were hit.

Taxidermy Tim suffered a good fall, but if he could stop the bleeding from his shoulder and side, he would survive. He hadn't broken any bones. He was damn lucky.

What he couldn't survive was what had dropped down from the window moments ago. They had thrown his Mother out of the house. She landed and broke into leathery pieces in a flurry of dust and mites.

They had desecrated his Mother's body. There was no way to repair the damage done. His first reaction was anger.

So why wasn't he crying yet? He should've been thrown into the deepest pits of despair. She was the last member of his family. She supported him and encouraged him throughout everything.

The bitch also told him what to do. Mother was a bossy, bossy bitch. He was a man, not a child. He was sick of being treated like he couldn't handle his emotions. He could make decisions without her chiming in with her two cents. The bitch. Oh, the dead bitch.

Mother wouldn't let him touch the women. Tim worked extra hard to form bodies made up of only the honest-to-God good parts. She always said he had failed after each of his attempts. That there was too much bad mixed in with the good. He wasn't anywhere near as good at the process as his father was.

Mother lied. He knew the process fine. He was a craftsman. He was damn good at his work. The truth was she didn't want him to fall in love and leave her alone on this island. Loneliness made her lie. Mother was selfish.

He could carve up and mold the women any way he damn well pleased from now on. This time, he would skip the "good" parts. He would target the nastiest parts. The dripping with evil parts. He never told Mother he enjoyed the nasty bits the best. They brought him the most pleasure.

He enjoyed having sex with one of the sculptures he created about six months ago. If only Mother hadn't interrupted him. He was a virgin, and he was so close to an orgasm, but Mother, Goddamn Mother! She had to interrupt him. Talk about breaking his dick's back! His hard on shrank like a turtle head escaping back into its shell.

No more, Mother.

Let some wild creature chew your remains, and be gone with you!

Freedom meant one thing. He needed female parts for his slut sculpture. All he had to do was somehow get back inside the house, reclaim his cutting tools, and get to work.

Taxidermy Tim hid nearby.

His eyes didn't leave the house.

Once he had his chance, he would put together his perfect slut.

STOCKING UP

Bruce had become a director again in his own way. He was telling people how to survive. Whether he was qualified to do so or not, it didn't matter. Someone had to take charge.

The others were looking for weapons. He located two gas cans in the basement. One was full of gas, and the other was half full. He prayed the psycho's boat could get them home.

He was about to search upstairs when Zoe stopped him. She had taken the killer's hammer and hatchet. Her face was apprehensive when she approached him.

"Bruce, I just wanted to say I'm sorry I punched you earlier."

He had pretty much forgotten about the incident; especially up against everything else that had transpired. "Thank you for saying that. I probably deserve it. I'm in that kind of business. I can't pretend I'm a saint."

"It's no excuse. I had the wrong idea about what happened with my sister on your movie. Candy explained everything. My sister lied to me. You didn't do anything wrong. You're just doing a job."

"Apology accepted. I want all of us to get off this island and live long happy lives. Apologize by surviving. Apologize by going on and doing great things."

They shook hands.

"Deal."

From downstairs, Blast cheered from the first floor, "*Whoa yeah!*"

Bruce and Zoe hurried to meet up with the exuberant special effects man. Blast was inside a room on the first floor. Candy and Kate were also with him. The room was stocked from top to bottom with weapons. A pegboard was nailed up against the wall. M-16s, Mossberg pump action shotguns, .357 magnums, and elephant guns were hung from hooks. Even a box of hand grenades was stowed in one corner.

Everybody was arming themselves. Nobody cared where Taxidermy Tim got the weapons from. All that mattered was that the weapons were here.

Blast was stoked. "Now you're fucking talking. This gives us a fighting chance."

Kate was looking more and more determined the longer she was with the group. "I only want on that boat. I hate this island. It's going to take a lot of prescription drugs to erase the memory of this place."

"We all hate this island," Candy said. "This island can go to hell."

Kate eyed the group. "I've been meaning to ask you guys this. If Taxidermy Tim didn't bring you here, then why did you come here?"

The others looked at Bruce. Bruce smiled big. He shrugged. "Well. Okay. I'm a director. We were shooting a movie about a killer dinosaur. I shit you not."

"You what?" Kate's face went from tough bitch to amused. "No way. You're joking."

"We were supposed to be on a different island, but our captain took us to the wrong place. I swear it's the truth. Blast here is my special effects guy. Candy and Zoe are my lovely actresses. Everybody else on the crew, well..."

The conversation changed gears. Nobody was smiling anymore. Everybody wanted to leave in a hurry.

"I'm ready to go when you are," Kate said. "We'll find that path and go from there."

Bruce clutched both gas cans. "I'll carry these to fuel the boat."

Zoe gave up the hatchet and hammer for a 12 gauge. Candy, in all her bikini clad glory, was carrying an M-16.

Blast made his final choices. Two .357 magnums. "I'll carry my backpack. We'll put more ammunition in it. I threw in some jars and rags just in case we need to whip up some Molotov cocktails. God knows what we'll encounter out there."

"What happened to you earlier?" Bruce asked. "I lost you. I thought you were dead."

Blast sighed. "I'll tell you the truth, I got lost in the dust. That stampede blinded me every which way. I had to backtrack. That's when I saw the house again, and I ran in and blasted that creep to kingdom come."

"I owe you one," Kate said. "I owe all of you my life."

"Let's not get overboard," Bruce said. "We're in this together. You get us to that boat, all will be good. You can do me one favor, Kate."

"Anything."

"Load yourself with weapons up to the gills, and let's get out of here."

Kate grabbed a Beretta, a Rangefinder rifle with scope, and strapped two belts of grenades across her chest. "Okay. This bitch is ready to go."

Bruce gave her a thumb's up. "Sure looks like it."

Candy noticed the pad of paper on top of a pile of wooden crates. "What's this about?"

Bruce thumbed through the pages. "Huh. Looks like a bunch of lists. Food and weapons mostly." He stopped on the tenth page he flipped through and paused. "Interesting. Looks like

Taxidermy freak's father built up this small arsenal in case something from back home discovered them. The guy was planning on putting up a good fight if the police came knocking on their door."

Blast studied the steno pad. "I see the symbol for Blunt Taxidermy Services on the top corner. I can't imagine advertising taxidermy services on a pad of paper. It's not like they were a hotel or a real estate agent. And don't they advertise on sponges anymore?"

Zoe was chilled by a thought. "Could you imagine how long Tim would've gotten away with his crimes if we hadn't come along and stopped him? I'm so sorry, Kate. It's all so horrible."

Kate sneered. It was hard for anybody in the room to know what she was mentally processing. "He's dead. There's nothing anyone else can do now. How that family survived on this island for so long and why they did the things they did are all irrelevant. Sorry doesn't cut it. The victims will always be victims. That will never change. Revenge doesn't feel sweet, but escaping this damn island and doing something with my life, that makes me feel better. So let's move on. Please."

"Absolutely. I agree." Bruce studied everybody in the room. These people were ready for a new set of surroundings, and pronto. "Everybody good to go?"

Zoe gave Bruce a nod and clutched her shotgun. "I suddenly feel like I'm in one of your shitty movies."

"Very funny." Bruce was serious now. "I just pray for a happy ending."

Right after he said that, T-Rex smashed his head through the living room wall.

PART THREE

HOME INVASION

Bruce dared to glance from the edge of the hallway out into the living room. All he could see was the giant green head and those enormous teeth bite up a couch, bash a coffee table into smithereens with its forehead, and break the east wall into four pieces with a single blow with the side of its cranium. The nose kept sniffing for humans. Its hot nasty breath filled the house. He imagined being in a furnace fueled by halitosis wood.

Failing to locate meat, T-Rex shook its head back and forth in anger. The solid skull reduced wood to shattered debris. The living room was gone in seconds. The dinosaur was so exuberant in its biting, smashing, and bashing it didn't realize the upstairs was starting to come undone.

"Run out the back!" Blast shouted. "The house is coming down! Hurry!"

The two-story house collapsed from within. T-Rex was inside continuing to batter his way through the wreckage. With each stomp, shake of the head, and roar, its impatience only escalated. There was no calming the beast until blood was shed.

The group raced out to the backyard. They searched for any signs of the pathway Kate had mentioned earlier. It didn't take long to locate that path. The ground was well trod in a single line twenty yards leading out of the backyard. They followed the worn down grass to the edge of a thick forested area. There was indeed a fork.

Left or right? Which way would they go, Bruce wondered. One led to the boat, and the other...*death*.

Candy cried out, "What do we do?"

Zoe's eyes were wild. "Which way, Bruce?"

Bruce didn't want the pressure to decide. The situation didn't allow for hesitation. There was no way to make an educated guess. He simply had to choose.

"Left! Go left!"

Everybody followed Bruce. The forest was so thick he couldn't see more than a few yards. They stuck to the path. Blue and green monkeys were swinging from tree to tree around them. Others were jumping up and down and making shrieking noises of excitement.

"Shut up, monkeys!" Blast growled. "Those things are going to give us away. I always hated monkeys. I never found them funny in any context."

"We can't shut them up," Zoey said. "There's too many."

Trees were shoved aside with the ease of silk curtains. T-Rex was bounding forward at ramming speed. The dinosaur was knocking the monkeys out of the trees on his way. The monkeys were throwing coconuts at the beast. Each blow to the head enraged the dinosaur.

T-Rex had his revenge.

Monkeys were flattened by the monster's stomp and squish efforts. Growing crazier with bloodlust, the mouth chomped down on the top of a giant tree. Breaking up branches with its powerful jaws, some of the monkeys in those branches couldn't escape. Their bodies were squished and spurting blue blood. T-Rex's mouth was painted a neon blue for a moment before it swallowed their pieces whole.

The few monkeys that remained were smart enough to retreat.

The humans became the main target again.

Blast was quick to take action.

"Bruce, open one of those gas cans. Candy, dig into the backpack and hand me a rag. Zoe, fill one of the jars with gas. Kate, get my lighter from the side pocket. Ready yourself to light the Molotov cocktail. You're going to throw it at that big green dick bag."

Bruce and the group followed Blast's instructions. The special effects man knew how to create chaos on no budget or time, and this situation wasn't any different.

T-Rex was spitting out chunks of wood and random stones he'd picked up during his frantic monkey killing spree. Blue blood dribbled down its chin. Those demonic yellow eyes seemed to burn brighter with each new victim it devoured.

The group watched as it lowered its head, sucked in a breath, and came charging at them. Bruce was pouring the gas into the jar. Zoe was clutching it with shaky hands. Candy was tearing a rag into a smaller sliver. Candy jammed three quarters of the torn strip into the jar. Zoe closed the lid. Kate flicked Blast's lighter, lit the rag, and taking aim, hurled it at the incoming beast.

The group retreated up the path. The jar shattered. Bruce saw the glass break right between its eyes. Flames spread across its forehead. The smell of cooking flesh hit the air instantly. He couldn't see T-Rex's features—only a great ball of flames.

The dinosaur screeched in pain. It staggered in the other direction, flailing its head to fan the flames.

The beast was gone.

That was one problem solved.

Many more would soon show themselves up ahead.

T-Rex's attack had awakened the other predators in the woods, and they were about to pounce.

OPEN SEASON

Blast had both .357 magnums raised up at the forest. "Shoot everything in your way!"

From a cave entrance, a horde of green ticks the size of crabs skittered forth. They blanketed the ground in skirting green movements.

Kate removed two grenades from the belt slung across her front and hurled them towards the ticks. "Eat it, you ugly fucks!"

BOOM!

BOOM!

Half of the tick front was squashed by hot shrapnel. The ticks spilled gray guts in spurting and splashing fashion.

Candy and Zoe worked together on pouring another Molotov cocktail. They lit it up, pitched it forward, and caught the rest of the ticks on fire. They bubbled up and exploded against the raging heat.

A gathering of mega-sized wart hogs with tusks large enough to gore a person through three times over were fast approaching. Hooves kicked up curtains of dirt. Foam bubbled at the sides of their grunting and ravenous mouths. The dozens of eyes spread about their dark leathery bodies were bent in primal rage.

"What are you looking at, twenty eyes?"

Blast sent home a strong message to fuck off. The .357s did the talking. Tusks were shattered by bullets. Wart hog noses evaporated in giant clouds of red mist. Candy backed up the special effects man with a ream of M-16 fire. Hot pumping, shredding, penetrating bullets chopped them up into hunks of steaming would-be bacon.

"Keep going! Keep going! Keep going! Run!" Bruce encouraged them to cover new ground. They would tread so many yards only to be cornered by new threats. The forest refused to relent.

A daddy longlegs spider towered over the forest. The thin legs were so tall it could've matched the height of any big city skyscraper. The body was simply two circles of black meat covered in course hair. The eyes were a cluster of fifty oily black marbles that created one giant hideous eyeball. The mouth was a cartoonish slit.

The beast was about to lunge down upon them when T-Rex, burnt faced, leapt up and chomped its head off. The spider's face stump was leaking hundreds of gallons of black syrup and sludge down onto the woods. It pelted the trees. The group dodged the raining gore in horror. The reek tested their grit.

There was no time to vomit.

Only run.

The headless daddy longlegs tipped over on its side and collapsed. The concussion caused the group to all loose their footing and fall.

Stork looking birds with jagged beaks, raw meat jowls, and feathers that looked to be dipped in tobacco juice, were stirred from the trees.

Kate shouted, "Shoot 'em! Quick!"

Zoe's 12 gauge tore many of the hybrid storks into pieces. One flew down and pecked Bruce between the shoulder blades. Blast shoved his .357 into the bird's face and blasted its beak out its brains.

"You okay, mister director?"

"Yeah. Hurts like hell." Bruce dug into the backpack. He had a desert eagle pistol and started to play a very gory game of clay storks. *Now it's payback time!*

Zoe removed a grenade from Kate's belt and tossed it at another brave boar wanting a sample of raw human flesh. The grenade landed right beneath its belly and launched the boar up twenty feet into the air only to drop it back down as unrecognizable gore.

The grenade's blast had broken a pile of rotting logs and disturbed a snake's nest. These snakes were the size of boa constrictors. They were purple and black striped. Their faces split in two halves, revealing a wide maw of long teeth dripping with milky white poisons.

Candy pumped the mother snake with enough bullets to keep it down. The babies, roughly a foot long each, were slithering and threatening. They crawled up Zoe's legs, worked their way up her torso and arms, and pried their way into her mouth. She gagged and choked, trying to rip them from her mouth. Her efforts were useless.

Her throat bulged. Bones were shattered from within her body. Skin was ripping lengthwise from the pressure of the invasion. Her torso from her chest to between her legs was eaten through instantly. Her guts slopped out from her vagina in a hot mess. Snakes were audibly noshing on her insides.

Candy was horrified at the wet spaghetti sound of devouring. "ZOEY!"

12 gauge, Beretta, M-16, and grenade turned the scene into a cavalcade of dust and snake splatter.

Bruce knew their time was limited if they were going to survive. "We have to run for it. Go! Keep moving. Don't stop!"

Spiders the size of tanks and semi-trucks were skittering after them. Bats with glowing red eyes were hovering above them. A mix of vulture and reptile bird hybrids soon joined them.

"Our guns won't stop them. We have to get to that boat!" Bruce ran as fast as he could. He was lagging behind the group. He was the oldest and the slowest out of everybody. Blast stayed at the front shooting bullets to ward off any pending attack.

The spiders were coming in closer. They were right behind Bruce now. Any second, he would become arachnid chow.

Run, Bruce thought. *Keep running.*

If you die, maybe you'll buy them time to find that boat and escape. All that matters is that they live. It's my fault this is happening. All because of my stupid movie.

Bruce tripped and fell. He landed hard on the gas cans. "If the spiders get me, KEEP GOING! ESCAPE OFF OF THIS ISLAND!"

He didn't have time to get back up.

The shadows of his enemies were quickly upon him.

WITHOUT FEAR

Taxidermy Tim entered the woods without hesitation. He was armed with his instruments of death. His meat cleaver glistened with four different shades of bug guts. He dripped from head to toe with boar viscera, bits of grasshopper shell, neon blue monkey brains, and dead spider goo.

He followed the sounds of war to track his prey. The women, mostly. He wanted their good parts. He would make the sweetest, most voluptuous sculpture, and when that one rotted and ceased to satisfy his needs, he'd kidnap more women from the United States, and make another, and another, and another. He would never run out of flesh. He would never be satisfied. The future was bright with flesh to be cut and rendered into sexy shapes.

Taxidermy Tim crouched down when he heard the wild stampeding of hooves and paws and talons. The animals of the forest were mass retreating. He released himself from his crouch and knew he was in trouble. If the animals were running from something in the woods, how did the group of people fare? They could already be eaten, trampled into a useless mess, or had they had found his boat and escaped?

No. I can't lose them. They were perfect. Their breasts. Their skin. Their faces. Their pretty shiny hair. Everything was so right.

Tim was fleet-of-foot launching through the woods with nothing in his way to slow him up. Once he reached the apex of a hill, he immediately knew what had scared off the other animals.

He could see the towering tiger toad blow itself up. Out both of its sides, the skin bubbled. The thing was triple the size it was the last time he'd seen it. The toad was so huge, it could jump on a cruise liner and smash half the boat.

Tim's stomach sank. He noticed the group of people standing there yelling at each other. One was missing. Tim knew without having seen it happen what actually occurred.

You did this.

You swallowed up one of my women.

T-Rex wouldn't do this to me. I respected his turf, and he respected mine. You, TOAD, respect NOTHING!

He couldn't murder the toad himself. He wouldn't have to because on the horizon help was stomping its way over.

BATTLE ON

Candy forced Bruce back onto his feet.

"I'm not leaving you, old man. We either leave together or not at all. I'm not done living and neither are you."

Her fresh spattering of M-16 gunfire warded away the front of six spiders for mere seconds. Then her gun went dry. Blast cursed. He was also out of ammo. Kate had lost her Rangefinder when a collection of grasshoppers clutched onto and ate it down to its steel components. Kate was about throw two of her last grenades when something gargantuan shifted in the woods.

Bruce caught its enormous size. The amazing bulk was the size of an entire hill. Its orange, black, bumpy, and tiger striped body was overwhelming. He couldn't see what the thing was; he only saw what it could do.

A thick pink tongue much like six bungee cords combined sprang across the forest. The tip of the tongue stuck onto one of the spider's faces and ripped it right off. The tongue was a rapid fire weapon. *Flick-flick-flick-flick-flick.* The sticky tongue ripped thoraxes into bleeding fractions, pried off legs from sockets, and took down the fleet of giant spiders in seconds.

The other enemies in the forest fled at the sight of the superior beast. That left Bruce, Candy, Kate, and Blast as the only prey.

"We can't fight this thing," Blast said. "I think we made our best stand. I think we're fucked without lube."

Flick.

The tip of the neon pink stuck to Kate's head. The tongue retracted, lifting the horrified girl off of her feet. Her body soared across the forest over the tips of trees and was rolled up into the tiger toad's mouth. Her rising screams were suddenly rendered into silence. Gone forever. Dead just like that, Bruce thought.

Candy screamed, imagining herself in Kate's position.

Bruce wanted to console her. There were no words in the English vocabulary to soothe her fears. This wasn't a place for humans to survive. The monsters and beasts owned this island. That would never change, and this was the clear evidence.

"Okay, okay," Blast said to himself. "Think. We're not dead yet. Look. We don't have enough bullets to save ourselves. I say fuck it. Use those gas cans to light this forest up. Burn it down to the fucking ground. That'll buy us some time to get to that boat. Maybe."

"But we need the gas," Bruce argued. "There's a big stretch of ocean between here and back home."

"The boat's useless if we're being digested in that toad's stomach!" Candy growled. "I'm with Blast. Let's light this bitch up."

The night had set in without them realizing it. The sun was a fading ember on the horizon. Soon, the forest would be pitch black. Before anybody could comment further on their next move, the ground rumbled. Dirt started to sink and collapse around them. Something beneath them was rising up. Bruce grabbed Candy by the arms, and they jumped to the left of the forming sink hole.

Blast wasn't quick enough.

The hole didn't swallow him up.

What sprang out of the hole did.

Bruce watched the giant worm covered in glistening goop make his special effects man vanish. The mouth simply took him in whole. The worm remained in motion. It was mid-air, sailing high up above the tree tops. The immense body could've doubled as a sewer pipe. The worm curved its body about to come back down. The creature didn't have the opportunity to touch the ground.

Flick.

The tongue acted as a harpoon and stuck the worm through the middle. The worm thrashed, fighting the tongue's pull. It was jerked nearly a quarter of a mile and into the toad's hungry slit mouth. The loud SQUISH and SQUIRT of guts being forced out of skin echoed from inside the toad's cheeks.

Bruce hugged Candy close. "I love you. I was going to propose to you when this movie was over."

"What?" Candy's eyes went from overflowing with tears of terror to joy. "Really?"

"I promise you it's the truth."

Candy kissed him hard and hugged him close. "You still will marry me, Bruce Bruce." Through gritted teeth, "We're getting off this island. Let's burn this bitch down. We're getting to the boat. *I don't give a damn what's out there. They messed with the wrong porno bitch.*"

LIGHT THIS BITCH UP

Bruce and Candy opened both gas cans and began spreading the fuel around.   They worked fast spilling the noxious liquid everywhere.   Bruce flicked and set Blast's lighter to the ground. Whirling branches of flames spread instantly.   Yellow arms crawled up trees and caught dry timber on fire in seconds.   The process was alarmingly fast.   Treetops were pillars of raging flames. Everywhere was red with burning. Black smoke spread fast, ruining visibility.   The toad shrank away from the flames, doing two giant double hops and vanishing into the darkness of the forest.

The plan was to light up the woods and search their way through the dark. Now everywhere looked the same.   Which would should they go? he thought. Bruce would guide Candy one way, and fire would throw them in the opposite direction. They were doing circles.   Fire was everywhere.   They hadn't saved themselves. They had put themselves deeper into harm's way. Instead of being eaten, they would burn.

The prolific director imagined his life and career. He had seen tits by the mega pound. Sweaty sexual flesh displayed on camera for the fans to savor. Slasher killers chasing big breasted women throughout the woods with chainsaws, and axes, and hatchets, and strange knives. CGI beasts stalking dumb teenagers. He had spilled fake blood by the gallons. Up against the glory of his smut peddling career, he was standing beside his best friend and the woman he loved. He had achieved something, damn it, and it was great and wonderful, and nobody had a right to take it away from him.

"Come on, Candy! We've made it this far. I'm not giving up."

He could see a small break in the fire. They ran between two raging gulfs of flames to the other side. Fresh air hit them, and the two sucked in clean breaths with gratitude. Their eyes widened in surprise at what waited up ahead. The burning backdrop of the forest painted the beach in perfect light. There was a boat on the shore. All they had to do was jump on, start it up, and leave this nightmare behind them.

The happy moment ended.

Taxidermy Tim had snuck up behind Candy, wrapped one arm around her waist, and trained his thick cleaver up against her throat.

CREEPY TORMENTOR

"She's my flesh to mold and reshape. *Mine! All mine!* She's all nasty, and tasty, and sweet, and I like that. I'm going to enhance her body to accommodate my pleasures. I'm going to slide my carving tool deep inside that luscious body. I'm going to taste every inch of her, and I can't wait."

"You're done you sick fuck! Not another word from your sick mouth!"

Like a whip, Bruce lashed out at the crazy castaway. He twisted the man's wrist clutching the cleaver. The man didn't expect Bruce to fight back. Candy wriggled free and was behind Bruce. The director swung a wild and a successful punch to Tim's jaw. Decked, spewing a mix of blood and heavy saliva, the man struck the sandy beach. When the killer got back up to his feet and regained his senses, he was seething with animosity.

"The bitch is going to get it now. I'm going to do things to her alive, and then I'm REALLY going to do things to her when she's dead. Oh, her tits, and that sweet ass, and that sweet, sweet body. I'm going to play out every fantasy. I've built them up over decades. I'm going to show her a good time. She'll forget about you. There will only be me and my steel instruments. She'll be begging for death by the time I'm done with her.

"*Ohhhhhhh fuck!*"

The great tearing noise and the spraying of blood followed the pained shrill cry. The pink tongue landed on Taxidermy Tim's crotch. The tongue dug in three inches deep, and when it reared back with such force, it not only ripped his genitals from his body, it tore him in half from the stomach up to his head. The tongue flicked twice to pick up every piece of the killer.

One threat was gone.

The toad remained.

The enemy was on the beach, its body huddled close together as if it could either hunker down into the sand or use those back legs to spring at them. Those callous amphibious eyes bore into them considering when the exact right moment was to eat them. The toad was twice the size of the boat they sailed in on. They were nothing up against the enormity of the beast. They were unarmed and helpless.

"Maybe this really is the end," Candy sobbed. "We were so close to making it too."

Bruce agreed. He spilled his heart to her in those moments. There was nothing else for a man to say to his favorite woman when faced against impossible odds.

This really was the end.

He hugged the love of his life close and waited for unmerciful death to come.

KING OF THE ISLAND

"Bruce, look!"

"No fucking way!"

T-Rex sprang out of the burning forest. There was no stand-off moment or warning cry from the dinosaur. T-Rex was after his nemesis and was charging in full throttle. Bruce and Candy had to jump the other way to avoid being stamped into the ground.

The tiger toad was at the ready to fight for dominion. There would only be one king of the island. Before T-Rex could reach the toad, the pink tongue sprang forward. Instead of trying to snatch the dinosaur, the sticky part clutched onto T-Rex's cheek and ripped the green flesh from one side of his mouth. Half of T-Rex's teeth were visible and bleeding. The beast was enraged and undaunted by the ugly wound.

The toad shot its tongue again. T-Rex snatched the tongue like a rope, tensed its short but powerful arms, and swung the toad off the beach and into the air and spiked it onto the sand. Piss spat out its hind quarters in gushing fire hydrant spray. The toad lay there for a moment, blinked once, then rolled back onto its side, gathered back its stretched tongue, and poised itself for more fighting.

Bruce and Candy ran for the boat.

"Let's get to the boat. This is our last chance to get out of here."

Dinosaur and toad charged at each other. They kept butting heads again, and again, and again. Each of their faces were getting bloodier, angrier, nastier, and more determined. Who would let up first? The sickening thud of skull to skull wouldn't end. The beasts refused to relent.

Bruce and Candy climbed onto the boat. Bruce headed right for the steering wheel. He was about to turn on the motor and gun it the hell out of there.

One problem.

There was no key.

"Don't just stand there. Start this thing!"

"I can't. There's no key. Help me look for the damn key."

"What if it was on Taxidermy Tim's body?"

"Then we're screwed."

Together, they scavenged the boat for the prized key.

Tiger toad had used its back legs to thrust itself forward. It head butted the dinosaur in the chest. T-Rex gripped the toad when the blow struck, and they both splashed into the ocean. The wave created by their landing slammed into the side of the boat. Candy and Bruce had to hold onto something not to be pitched overboard.

The gladiators were trying to drown each other in the water. Web hands and clawed fingers pushed, dunked, shoved, and grappled for dominance. Both were causing enormous waves in the ocean non-stop.

"Why won't they hurry up and kill each other?" Candy griped. "Wouldn't that be great?"

"With our luck, they'll become fast friends and get us both instead."

"Shut up! Don't say that."

T-Rex had the toad by the back foot. He launched the toad back onto the sand. The toad lay belly up, temporarily stunned. That gave T-Rex plenty of time to stomp his way back onto land. T-Rex's snarl was that much more intense with half the skin of his face missing.

Tiger toad wasn't done fighting. The toad got back onto its haunches, took three hops, and stopped at a pile of broken up boulders. He sucked one boulder into its mouth. The toad blew up its body, creating giant air sacs at its sides. It used that air as force to shoot the boulder at his enemy.

The charging dinosaur dodged the first boulder with a tumble and a roll. The toad sucked in more boulders one after the other and shot three more its way. The dinosaur dodged one, punched the second into pieces, and was struck on the side by the final one. T-Rex skidded, throwing up sand in all directions. He was bent over, bleeding from a large gash across his chest. The dinosaur was breathing hard trying to regain his strength.

The boat was hit by several smaller pieces of boulder shrapnel. Bruce covered Candy's body to protect her. He watched the toad creep slowly towards the dinosaur. The toad was cautious and careful.

Bruce couldn't decide who he wanted to win. It would be fantastic if they both died, but the way they were carrying on, one would die before the other. So whose survival would benefit them the most? Maybe it wouldn't have to come down to that, he reasoned. All they had to do was find that key.

He kept looking.

The monsters kept fighting.

T-Rex was slumped on his side unmoving. The toad was inches away from his enemy. The toad nudged the dinosaur with its head.

"Is that thing checking if it's dead?" Candy asked. "This whole thing is insane."

When she said the word insane, the toad puts its front two hands on the dinosaur's back and lifted its head up in the air as if to claim its king status.

The toad made a big mistake.

T-Rex wrapped its tail around the toad's neck and grabbed the other end of his own tail to create a sort of rope and choked the toad. The toad's face shrank, and its eyes bulged. The toad's mouth was forced permanently open as it made strange *gaaak* noises. The dinosaur watched his enemy writhe with a sick primordial pleasure.

T-Rex was grunting and growling as it hurt its own body to do more damage to its nemesis. The toad's head kept vibrating harder and harder. Its mouth opened wider, gasping as the life was being squeezed right out of him. Squeezing back more and more, the toad's left eye popped out of its socket like a kid's pop gun. The orb dangled on a long cherry strand of orbital tissue. T-Rex bent forward and chewed and swallowed the eye.

In the beast's insane lust for bloodshed, it had made a mistake. Shifting forward to eat the eye allowed the toad to slip free from under the tail, make its body smaller, and escape.

The fight raged anew.

The toad sprang with its powerful back legs and punched the green tower in the sides ten times. T-Rex spat out blood and covered the beach in giant splashes of red. Winded, weakening, and desperate, the dinosaur sidestepped to the forest and ripped a flaming tree from its deep roots and swung it like a baseball bat. The tree smacked the toad in the mouth, forcing tracks of skin off of its face. Part of its sinus cavity could be seen through spurting processes.

The toad shot out its tongue, grabbed the burning tree, and launched it into the ocean. The tree shot over the boat. Bruce and Candy had officially stopped looking for the key to watch out for their safety and to be spectators to the amazing battle.

That show was nearing its finale.

The toad had regained a new shot of adrenaline. The tongue flicked twice. Each flick removed an arm. T-Rex stood there with bleeding arm stumps. The toad swallowed each arm whole. T-Rex was stunned, gushing out blood, and unable to move.

Tiger toad blew up his body like a balloon. The thing was five times its size now. Bloated and insane, tiger toad braced itself for a giant meal. One great FLICK later, the tongue wrapped around T-Rex's body four times, squeezed him tight, and lifted him off of his feet.

In four seconds, tiger toad's mouth shot open and unhinged like the entrance to some great castle. T-Rex went right down the toad's expansive throat and was gone.

Tiger toad.

Winner.

NOT SAFE YET

Candy located the keys.   There was a small hidden compartment in the boat's floor for a stashing place. Bruce was about to use that key to start up the engine when he noticed he was being watched. The toad was on the beach with its head turned at them. Its body was noticeably larger. Much of the forest was burning behind the monster. He wondered if the entire forest was going to be turned to ash by the time the blaze burned itself out.

"What's it doing?"

Candy's question was obvious. He didn't tell her that. He wanted his last moments in this world to be as pleasant as possible.

"It's waiting for the right moment to spring at us."

"Start the boat."

"If we start the boat, it might go after us."

"It's going to go after us anyway."

The simple movement of inserting the key into the ignition caused the toad to take one antsy step closer.

"Shit."

"Okay. Don't move. My bad."

"Figures it would happen this way."

"What do you mean?"

"I made movies where people were eaten by things like this though never a toad. I'm atoning for my sins. I made porno. I lived like a scumbag."

"Just because you made porn doesn't make you a scumbag. You're not a scum bag."

"I'm just saying; this situation is poetic justice."

"Fuck poetic justice. You're a good man. I love you. You're my husband. Fuck this toad!"

Candy reached into a compartment beside the wheel and fired a flare gun right at the toad. The flare landed inside the open track of its sinus cavity. The whole toad's head lit up a bright incendiary cherry. The toad scrambled, hopping left and right, and tripping over itself to put out the flare.

"Good work!"

"Just get us the hell out of here."

Bruce turned the key, and the engine came right on. They were speeding off and were a safe distance away when they noticed the toad on the beach with the backdrop of burning forest behind it.

Candy was screaming. "Oh my God! Oh my God!"

The toad's great belly was torn in twain. T-Rex's body lunged from the parted flesh curtains and dangling tubes of guts and organs. The dinosaur tossed aside the dead toad's body by kicking it. Its skin was melting from super powerful digestive enzymes. Chunks of flesh, meat, and bone were disintegrating fast. T-Rex didn't care. It threw its battle ravaged skull back and roared its dominance across the entire island and far out into the ocean. The glorious moment ended seconds later when T-Rex fizzled to death against the sand.

SAFE?

Bruce guided the boat into the ocean. Hours has passed, and the inklings of dawn were coloring the horizon. It was then the boat ran out of gas. They were fortunate because there were more gas reserves inside the boat in another hidden compartment.

When morning was in full force, Candy broke the long held silence between them. "What are we going to do?"

"What do you mean?"

"Everybody's dead. The cast and crew. We're going to have to tell the police. When we do that, what in the world are we going to tell them?"

"Nothing they'll accept as the truth. We can show them the island. I think that'll be proof enough. They'll never believe a word of what we tell them without something to back it up.

"There's one thing I am worried about. When news of this hits, those who died on that island will be exploited. They'll use the tragedy to market the film. You won't finish the movie, right?"

"Of course not. That doesn't mean the company won't find some other idiot to slap together a collection of scenes and call it *Dino Buffet 3*."

"So what's going to happen to us?"

Bruce regarded her scared face. "Nothing, honey. We didn't commit any crimes. Everything's going to be okay. Don't be afraid, Candy. I'm here. We're alive. Nothing can harm us anymore."

Something pricked him on the side. He turned to his hip and saw the dart sticking out. Where had it come from? Candy was already on the floor sprawled out and unconscious. His vision blurred. Everything in his body went weak. He slumped down onto the floor alongside his girlfriend as the tranquilizer dart did its job.

EPILOGUE

Bruce came awake in a small tiled room with a metal, cot a toilet, and sink. He was hazy and blinking the double vision out of his eyes. Whatever drug was shot into him, it was intense. He tried the door. Locked.

He pounded his fist against the door. "Hey! Where am I? Where's Candy? Who are you people?"

He heard steps approach. A confident and cool voice said, "Mr. Ryder, can I count on you to be calm when I open this door?"

"Where's Candy? What did you do with her? You can't hold people like this. We're Americans. We have rights. I'm going to sue your ass!"

"Whoa, Mr. Ryder. Candy's perfectly safe. She woke up before you. We're taking good care of her. What we need you to do is calm down so we can talk. Can you do that?"

Bruce's heart rate had spiked. He bent over the sink, splashed cold water on his face, lapped up a handful of water, and leveled out his breath.

"Mr. Ryder? Are you okay in there?"

"Yeah. I'll be calm."

"Very good."

The door opened. Candy shot into the room and hugged him. She was dressed in military fatigues. Her blonde hair was put back in a bun.

"What's going on here?"

"The Colonel will explain everything."

"The Colonel?"

"Call me Colonel Painter."

Bruce stuck his hand out to shake. "Nice to meet you. I didn't realize this was a military situation."

The Colonel was an old man with a gray flat top haircut and a face with more wrinkles than a Shar-Pei dog. He was built like a wall of bricks. His handshake was firm enough to break his wrist if the son-of-a-bitch felt so inclined.

"Your lovely friend here filled me on all the details. Let's go to a private room for a word."

Bruce didn't like the sound of that. But Candy wasn't scared. Relief kept playing out on her face. She locked arms with him and patted his chest. "It's okay. They're the good guys."

"Yeah. If that's true, why did you dart us on that boat? I didn't see you coming. It's clear you snuck up on us. Where are we, Colonel Painter?"

"All in good time. Keep following me."

Colonel Painter guided them down a narrow white hallway into a conference room. Inside was a table with a buffet of food.

"Go ahead and eat, Mr. Ryder. You need to replenish your energy."

"For what? You brought us here for a reason, and now you're about to unload some serious shit on us."

"Serious, yes. Go ahead and eat. Please. We're getting ahead of ourselves."

The colonel crossed his arms and stood there until Bruce loaded a plate with chicken, macaroni and cheese, and a side of green beans. He was hungry. Candy sat next to him at a small table. She was Velcro'd to his side.

Once he was done eating, the colonel lit a cigar, and enjoyed a pull. He let the smoke crawl out of his lips.

"No matter what I say, hear me out first. You found that island on accident. Yes, we know about the creatures there. We've been researching them and doing tests over the years. We mined every scientific piece of information from that place. We weren't sure what to do with the island after that, so we left it alone. It was guarded for many years, then we had to pool our resources elsewhere. A new global threat has taken up all of our energies. We're understaffed. You getting on that island was a masterful fuck up. Somebody would've stopped you, but we haven't had surveillance on the island for awhile. I know, it makes us look like a bunch of assholes. Point noted.

"That said, you burned down that entire island. The fire is what brought us there, and why we picked you up. We shot you with darts to avoid resistance. We weren't sure if you were armed or if you were half out of your minds from what you witnessed. It saves time getting you from point A to point B if you're unconscious.

"Moving on, I'm in charge of a special branch of the government. I work for the AGCG. That stands for the Anti Globo Corps Group. Globo Corps has turned into a powerful terrorist superpower. These terrorists aren't the bomb in your shoe variety. They've already tried to destroy us with their battle whale."

"Battle whale?"

"Let me finish, Mr. Ryder."

Candy was holding him tighter. They were both nervous. The food in Bruce's stomach was being painfully digested. He was sweating now. Everything about the situation felt so wrong.

"Globo Corps used to be a corporate super power. They made normal garden variety products like your lawnmowers and tampons. Innocent enough. But now they want to take over the world. I'm talking about complete world domination. It's something right out of one of your movies, Mr. Ryder, and I'm not talking about the pornos.

"Globo Corps has created a new brand of weapons. They already have missiles, soldiers, high tech weapons, and the funding to pull off their plans. The one thing that worries us the most is what else they have."

Both Candy and Bruce said, "And that would be?"

"*Monsters*."

Bruce was shaken. "Monsters? Did I hear you right?"

"Hell yes, you did. They have monsters beyond your wildest imagination. Things with tentacles, and scales, and big ass teeth. I can go into the details later. Imagine your worst nightmare blown up to mega proportions. That would be the humble beginning of what we're up against. There is one thing Globo Corps wasn't counting on."

"And what was that?" Candy asked softly.

Colonel Painter had a knowing smile plastered across his face. The bastard was thoroughly enjoying this session. "We've got a team of some of the best operatives the government has ever had the pleasure of utilizing. I'm talking about Anchor Stevens, Freddy Stones, Pierce Range, and Nick Folder. We've got other operatives up our sleeves too. These are the best of the fucking best. They will serve our cause well."

"I don't know who any of these people are, Colonel." Bruce couldn't shake that horrible sinking feeling. "Why tell us any of this information? Please, this conversation is killing me. Why do you need us at all? We make movies."

"Oh, you'll understand things very soon. There's also another X factor these Globo Corps goons weren't counting on that you should know about."

"Yeah," Bruce said. "What else you got? A nuclear sling shot?"

The colonel was unfazed by the bad joke. "No. The thing they weren't counting on is that we have monsters too."

"*Whaaat?*" Bruce felt himself go limp in his chair. "This is so unbelievable. I don't know how we can help you. I really don't."

"I'm getting to that, and hey, what do you know? We're about to arrive to the point of this talk. That island you torched is all ash. That was a piece of government property you destroyed. That's a big no-no. We're talking about serious jail time."

Bruce struck his fist against the table. "We were defending ourselves! There were things on that island you can't imagine. I think self-defense applies here and then some!"

Colonel Painter moved swiftly to grab Bruce's pointer finger. He pulled it backwards and almost broke his finger.

"Oh God! Stop!"

"Let him go!" Candy shouted. "Okay. We'll listen to whatever you have to say. He's sorry. Now stop it."

The colonel released his finger. He enjoyed his cigar for a moment as Bruce was bent over clutching his hand in agony.

"Moving on. Yeah, you destroyed some government property. We can go on about what you had to do and why you did it, and it wouldn't change a thing. The point is, you can either go to jail, or you can serve your country. Those are your options. And know this, you don't get a lawyer. This is deep secret government stuff. When it comes to this brand of terrorism, all rules are thrown out the window. Our backs are up against the wall here."

Bruce looked into Candy's face. They both knew they had no choice but to go along with the colonel's wishes.

Bruce answered for the both of them. "What is it you want from us?"

"It's simple. I want you two to video document our battle with Globo Corps. We're going to an undisclosed location in the Middle East. That's where they're keeping their monsters trained to attack the United States. The plan is to attack their base, take out the threat, and save the day. We want you to record every moment. Call it the government covering their asses. Say it's for insurance reasons. Whatever. After the war in Iraq, we need clear evidence of the threat we're terminating. Otherwise, it'll look like we're just playing with our dicks, you get me?"

"I guess so," Candy said. "*Maybe*."

"Yeah, yeah, we got you." Bruce crossed his arms. "You're basically blackmailing us into doing what you want us to do. Whatever. This is a typical game of government chess. But we need some level of reassurance that if we do what you're saying, that once it's all done, we're free."

"Absolutely. You serve your country, you do your duty, you will return to your lives before all of this happened."

Candy blurted out, "How long do we go to jail if we don't? Just curious?"

"The jail sentence will be thirty-five years. At least."

"That answers that question," Bruce balked. "Give me a camera. Let's shoot this shit."

"Great, you're both in," the colonel said, smiling big. "You want to see something really cool before you're briefed on the mission and you meet the gang?"

They didn't answer.

The colonel didn't care. "Okay. Here we go."

They were following the colonel down several sets of stairs. It appeared they were on some kind of ship.

"Let me reassure you, you'll be with a group of soldiers that are topnotch. Real pros. Your safety will be number one."

Bruce held Candy's hand. They were both trembling. His life had gone from one extreme to another in a matter of minutes. The danger hadn't left their lives. They had fallen deeper into a bad place, and there was no turning back.

The colonel stopped in front of a steel door. Three soldiers armed with M-16s stood guard. They parted to let the colonel punch a code. When the door opened, Bruce and Candy's jaws dropped.

The colonel presented the contents of the room. "It's like from one of your movies, isn't it? And I'm not talking about the pornos."

Holy shit, was all Bruce could think. *Holy motherfucking shit.*

Candy's eyes were giant.

Inside towering glass cages, T-Rexes by the hundreds stood at the ready for battle. They were covered from head to toe in massive machine guns, rocket launchers, flame throwers, and new wireless technologies.

The colonel slapped Bruce on the back. "They're ready for their close up, Mr. Ryder! These dinos are only the beginning of our defenses. You should see the battle belugas." Bruce had to hold up Candy. Her legs nearly buckled from underneath her.

"Battle what?"

"Put your questions on pause, Mr. Ryder. I'm going to brief you two on what's going on very soon. Don't you worry. We're about to go to war in a matter of hours. *Globo Corps won't know what hit them.*"

CHECK OUT OTHER GREAT DINOSAUR THRILLERS

WRITTEN IN STONE
by David Rhodes

Charles Dawson is trapped 100 million years in the past. Trying to survive from day to day in a world of dinosaurs he devises a plan to change his fate. As he begins to write messages in the soft mud of a nearby stream, he can only hope they will be found by someone who can stop his time travel. Professor Ron Fontana and Professor Ray Taggit, scientists with opposing views, each discover the fossilized messages. While attempting to save Charles, Professor Fontana, his daughter Lauren and their friend Danny are forced to join Taggit and his group of mercenaries. Taggit does not intend to rescue Charles Dawson, but to force Dawson to travel back in time to gather samples for Taggit's fame and fortune. As the two groups jump through time they find they must work together to make it back alive as this fast-paced thriller climaxes at the very moment the age of dinosaurs is ending.

HARD TIME
by Alex Laybourne

Rookie officer Peter Malone and his heavily armed team are sent on a deadly mission to extract a dangerous criminal from a classified prison world. A Kruger Correctional facility where only the hardest, most vicious criminals are sent to fend for themselves, never to return.

But when the team come face to face with ancient beasts from a lost world, their mission is changed. The new objective: Survive.

CHECK OUT OTHER GREAT DINOSAUR THRILLERS

SPINOSAURUS
by Hugo Navikov

Brett Russell is a hunter of the rarest game. His targets are cryptids, animals denied by science. But they are well known by those living on the edges of civilization, where monsters attack and devour their animals and children and lay ruin to their shantytowns.

When a shadowy organization sends Brett to the Congo in search of the legendary dinosaur cryptid Kasai Rex, he will face much more than a terrifying monster from the past. Spinosaurus is a dinosaur thriller packed with intrigue, action and giant prehistoric predators.

LAND OF DEATH
by Eric S Brown & Alex Laybourne

A group of American soldiers, fleeing an organized attack on their base camp in the Middle East, encounter a storm unlike anything they've seen before. When the storm subsides, they wake up to find themselves no longer in the desert and perhaps not even on Earth. The jungle they've been deposited in is a place ruled by prehistoric creatures long extinct. Each day is a struggle to survive as their ammo begins to run low and virtually everything they encounter, in this land they've been hurled into, is a deadly threat.

CHECK OUT OTHER GREAT DINOSAUR THRILLERS

JURASSIC ISLAND
by Viktor Zarkov

Guided by satellite photos and modern technology a ragtag group of survivalists and scientists travel to an uncharted island in the remote South Indian Ocean. Things go to hell in a hurry once the team reaches the island and the massive megalodon that attacked their boats is only the beginning of their desperate fight for survival.

Nothing could have prepared billionaire explorer Joseph Thornton and washed up archaeologist Christopher "Colt" McKinnon for the terrifying prehistoric creatures that wait for them on JURASSIC ISLAND!

K-REX
by L.Z. Hunter

Deep within the Congo jungle, Circuitz Mining employs mercenaries as security for its Coltan mining site. Armed with assault rifles and decades of experience, nothing should go wrong. However, the dangers within the jungle stretch beyond venomous snakes and poisonous spiders. There is more to fear than guerrillas and vicious animals. Undetected, something lurks under the expansive treetop canopy...

Something ancient.

Something dangerous.

Kasai Rex!

CHECK OUT OTHER GREAT DINOSAUR THRILLERS

THE VALLEY
by **Rick Jones**

In a dystopian future, a self-contained valley in Argentina serves as the 'far arena' for those convicted of a crime. Inside the Valley: carnivorous dinosaurs generated from preserved DNA. The goal: cross the Valley to get to the Gates of Freedom. The chance of survival: no one has ever completed the journey. Convicted of crimes with little or no merit, Ben Peyton and others must battle their way across fields filled with the world's deadliest apex predators in order to reach salvation. All the while the journey is caught on cameras and broadcast to the world as a reality show, the deaths and killings real, the macabre appetite of the audience needing to be satiated as Ben Peyton leads his team to escape not only from a legal system that's more interested in entertainment than in justice, but also from the predators of the Valley.

JURASSIC DEAD
by **Rick Chesler** & **David Sakmyster**

An Antarctic research team hoping to study microbial organisms in an underground lake discovers something far more amazing: perfectly preserved dinosaur corpses. After one thaws and wakes ravenously hungry, it becomes apparent that death, like life, will find a way.

Environmental activist Alex Ramirez, son of the expedition's paleontologist, came to Antarctica to defend the organisms from extinction, but soon learns that it is the human race that needs protecting.

SEVERED**PRESS**

CHECK OUT OTHER GREAT DINOSAUR THRILLERS

LOST WORLD OF PATAGONIA
by Dane Hatchell

An earthquake opens a path to a land hidden for millions of years. Under the guise of finding cryptid animals, Ace Corporation sends Alex Klasse, a Cryptozoologist and university professor, his associates, and a band of mercenaries to explore the Lost World of Patagonia. The crew boards a nuclear powered All-Terrain Tracked Carrier and takes a harrowing ride into the unknown.

The expedition soon discovers prehistoric creatures still exist. But the dangers won't prevent a sub-team from leaving the group in search of rare jewels. Tensions run high as personalities clash, and man proves to be just as deadly as the dinosaurs that roam the countryside.

Lost World of Patagonia is a prehistoric thriller filled with murder, mayhem, and savage dinosaur action.

SAVAGE ISLAND
by Alan Spencer

Somewhere in the Atlantic Ocean, an uncharted island has been used for the illegal dumping of chemicals and pollutants for years by Globo Corp's. Private investigator Pierce Range will learn plenty about the evil conglomerate when Susan Branch, an environmentalist from The Green Project, hires him to join the expedition to save her kidnapped father from Globo Corp's evil hands.

Things go to hell in a hurry once the team reaches the island. The bloodthirsty dinosaurs and voracious cannibals are only the beginning of the fight for survival. Pierce must unlock the mysteries surrounding the toxic operation and somehow remain in one piece to complete the rescue mission.

Ratchet up the body count, because this mission will leave the killing floor soaked in blood and chewed up corpses. When the insane battle ends, will there by anybody left alive to survive Savage Island?

www.ingramcontent.com/pod-product-compliance
Lightning Source LLC
Chambersburg PA
CBHW030535130626
46552CB00006B/2261